BOLLYWOOD SERIES

Double Take

Puneet Bhandal

FAMOUS BOOKS

Chapter 1

'I wasn't in Goa last week,' insisted Deepa. 'I was shooting in Mumbai. Hey, maybe it was my double!' she laughed. 'You know they say everybody has one.'

'Yeah, I've heard that old saying too, but it's really

odd,' replied Sara, Deepa's former schoolteacher. She had just bumped into her old pupil, who was laden with designer shopping bags, in Bandra Bazaar. 'My daughter swore it was you and she's seen you lots of times before.'

'Well, it was definitely somebody else. Probably someone trying to look like me.'

'Yes, that's quite possible. You're such a big star now, everyone wants to look like you,' complimented Sara. 'They all want your long, straight hair, especially my daughter.'

'How sweet!' chirped Deepa, flicking her lustrous locks aside. 'Who would have thought, hey? Do you remember how shy I was at school? And how unfashionable?'

'Yes, how can I forget?' Sara chuckled. 'You were pretty back then, but you had those two long plaits and you used to blush crimson when anyone even spoke to you! Who could have predicted this?'

Deepa swung her shopping bags around, pleased at the high praise. 'Well, it was my dad's wish really, the acting thing. It's been quite a struggle, though,' she revealed. 'My first two films didn't do that well and I thought my days were numbered. But thanks to the buzz created by *Mumbai Magic*, I'm getting plenty of good offers now. Dad's over the moon.'

'Yeah, I bet,' nodded Sara, as she looked around the busy shopping street to see if a taxi was available. 'The film's done so well. I really enjoyed it. And even though you had a smaller role than the other girls you really stood out.'

'Thanks!'

'No, I think I should be thanking you – I've now got a claim to fame,' joked Sara. 'I'm known as Deepa Khanna's schoolteacher!'

Deepa giggled happily, throwing her head up as she did so. She caught sight of a huge billboard carrying a publicity poster for *Mumbai Magic*. It was a well-recognised hoarding by now, providing a splash of colour to hundreds of cities, towns and villages across India.

A smaller version of the same print took pride of place in Deepa's living room at home. Her dad, Jayant, had bought a pretty ornamental frame for the still which featured Deepa standing alongside the famous stars that made up the film's cast, including Marc Fernandez, Ajay Banerjee, Bela and Monica.

Later that afternoon, as Deepa was lying idly on the sofa at home, she looked up at the poster again and considered it proudly. But then another thought occurred to her. 'Dad, do you think *Mumbai Magic* was a hit just because of the publicity generated by the fighting between Bela and Monica? Or do you think people genuinely liked the film?'

'Who cares?' he scoffed. He peered over the day-old newspaper he was reading.

'I was just wondering, that's all,' replied Deepa, disappointed at his nonchalant response.

'The fact that those two girls were having cat fights at the time of the release will certainly have helped. They were in the papers all the time and they must have attracted a lot of attention to the film, but at the end of the day, does it matter if that's why it was a success?' he rumbled on. 'There's no magic formula – some films work and some don't. Don't dwell on it. It's a hit and you're getting good offers – at last. That's all that counts. Take them while they're coming.'

'Yeah, I guess so, although–' but Deepa didn't even get a chance to finish her sentence before her father cut her off again.

'Just be glad that all the thousands of rupees we pumped into that stage school haven't gone to waste,' Jayant said, putting his newspaper down and crossing his legs. 'I tell you, I was getting really worried about the state of your career last year. It didn't look like you were ever going to bring any money into this house and I'd started to think it was time we married you off.'

Deepa watched as her dad picked up his newspaper and started reading it again. She shook her head, got up off the sofa and walked towards the door, glancing over her shoulder as she left the room. Her dad's attention was fully focused on the article; he didn't even notice that she had gone, let alone suspect that he may have hurt her feelings.

She walked silently out of the room.

'What's wrong, *beti*?' asked Deepa's mum, Shanta, as they passed by each other in the long, thin hallway.

'Nothing, Mum,' replied Deepa quietly. 'Dad's just trying to make me feel bad about the money stuff again. I've got a hit movie now and he's still not happy.'

'Aah! Don't be sad, Deepa,' said Shanta sympathetically. 'Just ignore him.'

'How can I?' challenged Deepa. She held her hands up in frustration. 'He has this way of making me feel bad about everything. Somehow, every time this conversation comes up, he makes me feel like an underachiever – and I hate it.'

Shanta followed Deepa as she walked towards the staircase. 'I'm sorry, Deepa. I wish he'd appreciate your success more. I don't understand him either…

I mean, you never even wanted to become a film actress… it was on his insistence that you ended up at stage school.'

'Yeah, and then when the fees needed to be paid, he'd always moan about it – I remember it well,' said Deepa, turning around and heading upstairs.

Jayant was a strong-willed, traditional male who felt he should make all the decisions for the household. He expected Shanta to stand back and go along with whatever he wanted, and after years of letting him have his way she didn't think she had it in her to suddenly start challenging him. Although Shanta felt guilty at not being able to defend Deepa at times when Jayant was criticising her, she desperately wanted her daughter to succeed, proving she did have what it takes.

Shanta slowly went up the stairs and, after a gentle tap on the door, stepped inside Deepa's bedroom.

'He means well, your dad,' she whispered, shutting the door softly behind her. 'He does love you. You know that, don't you, Deepa?'

Deepa grabbed a nail file from her dressing table and plonked herself down on her bed. She smoothed the file over her fingertips.

'He's desperate for you to earn good money

because he's seen hard times. *Really* hard times.'

Deepa looked up at her mum, her deep, dark eyes failing to hide the sadness she felt.

'Look, many Indian fathers are like this, darling,' Shanta continued as she sat down alongside Deepa. She took her daughter's hand and clasped it lovingly. 'They see a daughter as a financial burden – sad, but true. I want you to prove that you're worth your weight in gold. I know Sachin gets all the attention, but that's because he's only twelve, he's the baby of the family.'

'*And* he's a boy,' replied Deepa, raising her eyebrows. She smiled at her mum and gave her hand a gentle squeeze in appreciation of the moral support. 'I wish the world for Sachin too, Mum. He's my brother and there's no way I could be jealous of him. But I can't understand why Dad shows no warmth towards me. It's as though he's constantly disappointed in me and I can't do anything to please him. I don't know what I'm doing wrong.'

'You're not doing anything wrong.'

'Then why is he like this with me? I've started to achieve all the things he wanted, but his attitude still hasn't changed. So weird.'

Shanta looked at her daughter and moved

forward to kiss her forehead. 'You think too deeply about things,' she said, trying to sound more upbeat in an effort to lift the mood. 'Just keep busy in your work and try not to dwell on your father's habits. He can't really help himself, but he's not likely to change now, I'm afraid!'

Deepa smiled. She knew her mum was right.

'You're going to go far – I just know it,' continued Shanta, standing up. 'Talking of which, I think you'd better get ready. Aren't we supposed to be at the opening of that record shop at six o'clock?'

'Yeah, we are,' sighed Deepa, quickly getting up when she realised what time it was.

'Are you looking forward to it?' her mum asked.

'Mmm yeah, I guess. It's nice to be in demand for all these events but it's such an effort sometimes. Like now, for instance. I'm in too much of a bad mood to smile for the cameras!'

'That's life, Deepa. We need to learn to hide our true emotions sometimes. If we didn't, the world would be a terrible place,' said Shanta as she moved across the room to open one of Deepa's wardrobes. They were made to measure and so big and tall that they housed most of Shanta's clothes too.

'Which colour should I go for?' Shanta asked, getting down to business. She carefully selected a plum-coloured saree with gold embroidery. 'What about this one?'

'It seems a bit loud for a low-key place like a record shop. I think you'd be better with something more simple. Go for the pale yellow one, perhaps… that one at the end.'

'This one?' Shanta reached out for the more sober outfit.

'Yeah, it's nice.'

'Fine. You're probably right. Anyway, it's not about me,' she reminded herself. 'Off you go, madam. Your outfit's been ironed. Get dressed and I'll tell the driver to be here in half an hour.'

Deepa did as she was told and thirty minutes later, looking sublime in a cream-coloured *kameez pyjama* with red bead-work, she was standing outside the house with her mum, waiting for the taxi driver to arrive. He pulled up a few moments later and soon, they were on their way to the grand opening of a record shop owned by the producer of one of Deepa's forthcoming films.

'By the way, I don't think it's a good idea to tell your dad you're not getting paid for this,' Shanta whispered to Deepa in the back of the car. 'You know what he's like. He doesn't understand the concept of free, promotional work, and he'd probably just get angry about it.'

'Tell me about it!' Deepa said, rolling her eyes. 'All he ever wants to know is how much I'm getting paid this time. Crazy!'

Shanta shook her head. 'I think he should get himself a job in a bank or something like that. Then he'll finally be surrounded by the thing he loves the most!'

Mother and daughter laughed out loud, thoroughly enjoying each other's company, and in what seemed like no time at all, they'd arrived at their destination.

A queue of fans, eager to glimpse superstar Deepa Khanna and have a chance of getting her autograph, was snaking along the street. Some of her admirers were wearing Deepa T-shirts and one small girl was even dragging along a life-size cardboard cut-out of her.

The cars, taxis and bikes that trundled past were sounding their horns regardless of whether they needed to and street vendors in the neighbouring alleyways were shouting at passers-by, eager to grab some business. It was always busy in this part of town, and the presence of a superstar just added to the crowds.

Above the entrance to the record shop was a big

sign in blue neon lights that read: Javed's Audio Visual Cave.

'Cave! What a weird thing to call a record shop…' Deepa looked sideways at her mum with a slightly pained expression. 'Let's just get in and out fast. It's so busy here, it's gonna be mad,' she said, looking around. 'And Javed's a real chatterbox, so as soon as we're done, we'll have to make a run for it or we'll be here for ever.'

The taxi pulled up in a small alleyway and Deepa and Shanta got out, taking care their clothes weren't soiled by the muddy ground beneath their feet. Deepa tried to squeeze past a rickshaw to reach the side entrance that Javed had asked her to use and just as she was about to enter, a voice called out. 'Hey Deepa, remember me?'

She turned around to look at the rickshaw driver and saw a familiar face. It was Rakesh, a boy who had been in her class at primary school. 'Hi, Rakesh!' said Deepa pleasantly. 'How nice to see you after so many years! How are you? And your mum?'

'I'm fine, thank you. We all are… I have my own business now,' he told her, wiping the handlebars of his vehicle with a grimy leather cloth as he did so. 'Driving rickshaws, as you can see. But you… you're a star!' He beamed widely, showing his excitement.

'I've been waiting here for two hours, just hoping to see you.'

'Oh Rakesh, you haven't, have you? Now I'm really embarrassed,' said Deepa. 'It's so nice of you to make the effort. You must come straight in – you can't queue, it'll take for ever! Follow me. Do you remember my mum?' she added, extending her arm towards Shanta who was standing back while her daughter talked to her schoolfriend.

'Of course. *Namaste* Auntie.'

'*Namaste beta.*'

Still smiling broadly, Rakesh smoothed down his already neatly-parted hair and followed Deepa and her mum through the small door.

'Hello! Welcome Deepa, welcome Mrs Khanna!' boomed Javed, film producer and record shop owner. He opened his arms out wide as though he was going to hug both of them at the same time but then he caught sight of Rakesh, and his welcoming expression turned to one of alarm.

'Hey, hey, who are you?' he asked, halting Rakesh with an outstretched arm. 'Security – we've got an intruder!'

'No, no, he's an old friend of mine,' Deepa interjected. 'I just bumped into him outside and invited him in for a few minutes.'

'Oh,' replied Javed with disdain. He looked Rakesh up and down, taking in his neat but rather threadbare uniform.

'I saw Deepa's poster outside the shop and just wanted to see her again,' muttered Rakesh under his breath. 'We went to the same school. I was the first one here – my rickshaw's just outside, sir.'

'Okay, whatever... Everyone follow me,' Javed instructed as he led them inside. 'What do you think of the shop, Deepa?'

'The shop – or rather the cave – is beautiful,' she said, feasting her eyes on the extravagant decor. It was a lot better on the inside than the tacky exterior had led her to believe. Javed had covered the silver-painted walls with gold-framed prints of Bollywood publicity posters. Deepa focused on the one of *Mumbai Magic*.

'I'm glad to see you've got my film up there,' she told Javed. 'That's great.'

'Well, we wouldn't be inviting you here if you weren't famous, would we?' said Javed cheekily.

Shanta also beamed with pride as she looked at the poster which had pride of place amongst those of so many other classic films and Rakesh got his digital camera out and started taking photos of Deepa standing in front of it.

'Hey, don't you think you'd better ask the lady's permission first?' reprimanded Javed.

Rakesh's face dropped. He hastily shoved his camera back in his trouser pocket. 'Sss… sorry, Deepa,' he stammered. 'I just wanted to show my family and friends. Most of them don't believe I know you.'

'It's fine, Rakesh. You don't have to stop. Snap away to your heart's content,' she said, slinging her handbag over the back of a chair. She giggled and struck a few poses especially for him and he clicked happily away again.

Once Rakesh had got all the photos he wanted, Deepa looked out to the street through the shopfront and noticed the crowd outside had got sizeably bigger.

'Okay Javed *sahib*, what's the plan?' she asked. 'We'd better get on with it. People have been waiting for some time. What do you want me to do?'

'Just smile and look pretty,' he answered, laughing at his chauvinistic idea of a joke. But seeing that Deepa didn't find it so funny, he then pointed to a long, silver table and added, 'You can sit here and sign the DVDs and CDs people buy, but first we're going to inaugurate the place. We'll open the front doors, wait for the photographer to take a few snaps, and when you're ready, cut the ribbon that's tied outside. Which reminds me, where are the scissors?'

He looked around, suddenly frantic. 'Chandu! Go and get the scissors from upstairs and tell the photographer Deepa Khanna is here. He must have finished his tea by now!'

Shanta decided to take a seat at the far end of the record shop to keep out of the way, and Deepa edged her way to the front with Rakesh following closely behind her.

Deepa waved to a large group of fans through the closed glass doors and they cheered for her in return.

'Right, everyone,' Javed shouted out to his staff who were impeccably dressed in white shirts, red waistcoats and blue trousers. 'It's time to open up shop.'

Two burly security guards moved forward to open the doors and the crowd roared with delight. 'Deepa! Deepa!' screamed a few of her fans. 'Look this way, please!' shouted one young girl. As Deepa complied, a small silver camera flashed to grab a personal photo of the sparkling screen heroine.

Javed stood beside Deepa and after clearing his throat, announced, 'Ladies and gentlemen. Thank you very much for attending this auspicious occasion – the opening of Javed's Audio Visual Cave!'

Deepa tried not to think about the name of the shop – it made her want to giggle – and, tying her chiffon *dupatta* into a knot behind her so it wouldn't get in the way, she concentrated on cutting the ribbon. There was more applause as she snipped it and the two halves floated to the floor, and then the crowd began to edge forward, eager to get closer to Deepa and to see what goodies were in store.

'The lovely Deepa will be signing CDs and DVDs of her movies, so please form an orderly queue,' announced Javed loudly as Deepa rushed back into the shop, quickly taking a seat at the table that had been set up for her.

Over the next hour Deepa smiled and chatted away as customers eager to have the chance of a one-to-one moment with her hurriedly bought any product which featured her on the cover – including copies of her first two movies which had been dismal flops at the box office.

'Thank you,' said one little girl in plaits as Deepa handed her a signed copy of a DVD.

'You're very welcome,' said Deepa politely.

'I love your movies,' the girl gushed as she clutched the DVD, her eyes fixed on her idol's face.

'Come along, come along now!' shouted Javed impatiently. 'The queues are building up. Deepa, can you sign more quickly and move on to the next person, please?'

The girl blushed and gave Javed a moody glance before stomping off, her plaits swinging angrily behind her.

'And your name is?' Deepa asked the next customer. It was a teenage boy.

'Is that your idea of a joke?' he spat out.

Deepa, who had been looking down as she busily signed a copy of the CD he had thrust into her hand, looked up. 'Excuse me?'

'So you don't know who I am?'

'I'm afraid not,' she replied, failing to work out the young man's aggressive tone. She looked intently at his face. 'Were you at my school too? Like Rakesh over there?'

'What brilliant acting!' The boy started clapping. 'Hey guys, quickly get the signature of India's best, most convincing actress. She says she doesn't know who I am…'

'What's going on here?' asked Javed who couldn't understand why the queue wasn't moving. He soon realised the young man was causing the hold-up. 'What's your problem, kid? Get your copy signed and move to the till, please,' he called out, trying to remain calm but feeling hot under the collar.

By now people outside were tapping impatiently on the window, wondering why it was taking so long to get into the shop.

'My problem is,' began the aggrieved youngster, 'that this young lady was kissing me last week, but now, all of a sudden, she claims she doesn't know who I am!'

'What?' exclaimed Deepa, standing up quickly. Her cheeks went bright red and she stammered: 'Wh..wh.. what are you talking about? I've never even seen you before!'

'What did he say?' asked Shanta, hurriedly making her way to the front of the shop. She had almost fallen asleep in her chair but somehow, the word 'kissing' had snapped her out of her semi-conscious state.

Javed looked at Deepa, then at the boy, and then at Shanta. 'Right, security!' he screamed. As soon as the words left his mouth two guards emerged from a door at the side of the shop and grabbed the boy's arms.

'Get off me!' he yelled, his long, wavy hair flapping around. 'It's true! She told me she loved me but I should have known it was a lie. Girls like her are all the same – today they're yours, tomorrow somebody else's!'

Deepa raised a hand to her mouth in shock while Shanta looked at her daughter, horrified. The customers in the shop, however, were loving the real-life drama unfolding before their eyes – they'd certainly got their money's worth. Rakesh was probably the only one who looked concerned for Deepa.

'Mum, I swear I don't know him! Honestly!'

'If he's lying, don't let him get away with it, slap him!'

A few girls in the crowd giggled.

'Aunti*ji*, please come and sit down again,' urged Rakesh, sensing that he needed to take Shanta aside. He took her arm and guided her to the back of the shop, much to Deepa's relief.

'Sorry about that, Ladies and Gentlemen,' Javed said to the enthralled spectators. 'The young man is obviously a touch overwhelmed by meeting our beautiful star. I'm sure he'll be all right after a little sit-down. Now, who's next?' he asked, trying to smooth over this embarrassing and potentially damaging incident.

The crowd started moving forward again and for a few minutes, Deepa kept her head down and signed copies without making eye contact with anyone. Some of the people coming into the store didn't know exactly what had happened, but Deepa was still feeling awkward and confused. The young boy's outburst had seemed so genuine – as though he really did think he knew her – but Deepa was certain she had never met him before, let alone kissed him.

When Deepa finally dared to look up, she saw the boy through the window. He was on the other side of the road, still arguing with the security guards. His arms were flailing around as he continued to protest his innocence, and passers-by were stopping to see what was going on. The boy's face was so red and his look so intense that Deepa was sure he either really did believe he'd been dating Deepa or he was just plain mad.

Deepa's heart sank. The road to stardom was a very bumpy one indeed.

Chapter 2

'I think you look great with curly or straight hair,' said Deepa's stylist, Amrita, busy at work in her home-based beauty salon.

'I prefer it straight, though. Curly hair's a nightmare to manage, isn't it?'

'Well, it can be,' Amrita replied, feeling the thickness of Deepa's hair to gauge what it would look like piled high on her head. 'Now, I'm wondering what we should do with it today. You have to look glam for the TV interview tonight, but first we need to decide on a style for the daytime. The *FilmGlitz* fashion editor told me to keep it simple for the photo shoot.'

'Oh, okay,' replied Deepa. She wasn't that fussed. 'Whatever you think.'

'We can start with it loose… perhaps with just a clasp, and then you can get super glam with an up-do later on,' Amrita suggested. 'You want to knock 'em dead on TV. A lot of people watch *India Tonight*, especially since Mike Malik took over as host.'

'Yeah, I know. That's why his female guests always look stunning.'

'And have you seen how Mike flirts with them all? He's terrible!'

'He is, you're right,' agreed Deepa, laughing. 'Personally, I think he's a bit creepy. He'd better not get fresh with me. Although,' she added dreamily, 'if he was as gorgeous as Ajay Banerjee, for example, I wouldn't mind at all. In fact, I'd be well in there!'

'Ooh, Deepa, your secret's out now,' said Amrita, raising her right eyebrow. 'I could make some money out of this little revelation you know!'

'No! You mustn't,' squealed Deepa as Amrita began straightening her hair with the tongs. 'Anyway, it's hardly breaking news – who doesn't fancy Ajay?

He's so cute,' she gushed. 'When we were filming *Mumbai Magic,* I thought he was gonna go for Bela, and I was madly jealous! She is gorgeous, though, isn't she?'

'She is… but she's so nice at the same time… it's enough to make you sick! But do you think something has gone on between her and Ajay?'

'No, not as far as I know,' Deepa stated. 'I think he's single – which is why I'm so excited today. Me and Ajay being photographed for the cover of *FilmGlitz* – amazing, hey? And then I'm going to be working on a Vijay Kaul movie with him too. We're shooting in Goa at the end of this month.'

'Oh?' Amrita spritzed strong-hold spray and finishing shine on to Deepa's hair and then continued, 'So is the producer providing you with a stylist or have you found yourself a new one?'

'Oops! Sorry!' exclaimed Deepa, clapping a hand to her mouth. 'Honestly, it just slipped my mind. I was meant to ask you. Are you free to do it? I think it's ten days. I have to double-check the dates, but I promise I'll let you have them by tomorrow.'

'Excellent,' laughed Amrita. 'I am free at the end of the month, actually. It should be fine. Shoots in Goa are such fun, I did one last year. We worked all day and then partied all night on the beach. It felt like a holiday, but then I needed another one at the end just to catch up on my sleep!'

'Yep, I've heard it's a great place. I've never been,' said Deepa, while Amrita picked up a bright blue sparkly hair slide. 'My dad never took us anywhere when we were younger. He's so tight-fisted, we've never even had a family holiday together! I can't wait to go.'

'What do you think of the hair slide, Deeps?'

Deepa looked at herself in Amrita's huge mirror which had light bulbs set all the way around the frame. 'Yeah, I like it. Thanks Amrita, that's great.'

'You're welcome, darling. That's you done for now, but I've got someone else coming in a minute so I'll see you at the TV studio later. Have fun at the photo shoot.'

'See you,' said Deepa, air-kissing her. She made her way out of Amrita's house and jumped into the car that was waiting to take her to Foxy Photo Studio.

It was only a short distance away and Deepa arrived with a few minutes to spare. Taking a seat in the reception area, she decided to send one of her old schoolfriends a text message.

`'Got hot photo shoot with Ajay B for Filmglitz! Beat that! Deepa X'`

As Deepa threw her mobile back into her bag, she beamed from ear to ear at the thought of Rama's face when she read the message. Rama had really rich parents and always used to taunt Deepa about her family's latest holiday to Mauritius or Switzerland or wherever. Well, the shoe was definitely on the other foot now.

Two seconds had barely passed when Deepa's phone bleeped. A text message read: `'You cow! Hate you! Give that sexy hunk a smacker from me!'`

Deepa laughed out loud.

'Must be really funny, can I have a read?' came a voice.

Deepa looked up and was shocked to see Ajay standing right in front of her. 'Erm… no, no it's nothing, just girlie stuff,' she muttered, quickly slamming her phone shut.

'Girlie stuff, hey? Now I definitely want to know!' he joked, forcing her to break into a smile. 'How are you, Deepa?'

'Fine thanks,' she replied, thinking how lucky she was to have a moment alone with her dream man. 'Really chuffed that *Mumbai Magic* did so well. I've been keeping busy – for a change.'

'Well, you're a big name now, Miss Khanna,' he

complimented. 'Shall we go?'

Deepa rose from her seat and the pair began making their way to the studio. Ajay continued, 'Yes indeed, the sky's the limit for you now.'

'Well, we'll see,' she said modestly. 'Let's just take it a step at a time.'

'Your next step is getting steamy with me in this photo shoot. *FilmGlitz* wants to create a bit of a stir with this cover. The mag's out to shock,' he winked.

'Really?' Deepa looked worried. She'd been teasing her friend Rama about it being a 'hot shoot' but she was now praying it wouldn't be. 'My agent told me it was going to be a run-of-the mill image.'

'It is… you obviously haven't seen the film magazines lately,' grinned Ajay. 'I'm just off to talk to someone upstairs. See you in the studio in a few minutes. It's that door up ahead on the left.'

Ajay strode off and Deepa stood and watched him, discreetly admiring his muscular physique until he had disappeared around the corner. She then made her way to a room with 'STUDIO' written above the door. She entered nervously, wondering what she would have to do during this photo shoot. Ajay's joke was playing on her mind.

Deepa looked around. The photographer, Suraj Chandwallah, was carefully cleaning a camera lens.

'Hello,' said Deepa.

'Hi.'

'I'm Deepa Khanna. I'm here for the *FilmGlitz* cover shoot. Ajay's just gone to see someone and will be back in a few minutes.'

'Right.'

Deepa carried on looking at the celebrated snapper's face, waiting for him to add anything more to his one-word sentence, but he didn't, and just continued tending to his equipment.

'Ermm,' muttered Deepa. She coughed to clear her throat. 'Can I ask a question? I just want to know exactly what this shoot will involve. Ajay mentioned the word "steamy". I… I guess I need to know what that means.'

'Ha ha!' Suraj laughed as he placed his camera carefully on a huge white desk. Then he removed a packet of cigarettes from his pocket, took out a cigarette and lit it. 'You must be very new to this industry. That's not the question of a seasoned pro…'

Deepa blushed. She didn't say a word for a few moments, but then she gathered her composure, straightened herself up and looked Suraj straight in the eye. 'I don't care if I seem naïve,' she said boldly. 'I need to know what we're doing before we start. You must have been briefed by the editor – I'm sure you can answer my question quite easily.'

Suraj, who was now sitting on the table and blowing smoke rings in the air, was surprised to hear her fire back at him in this way, but before he could reply, Ajay waltzed into the room.

'Ready to go, guys?' Ajay asked, clapping his hands eagerly. He looked around the nearly empty room. 'Hey, where is everyone?'

'Just another few minutes, Ajay. Our stylist will be here soon and the rest of the team are around, probably having a coffee next door. You can both take a seat there,' said Suraj, pointing to a small waiting area. 'I've got a couple of details to check then I'll be with you.' Suraj stubbed his cigarette out and then went out to make a call on his mobile.

Deepa was annoyed at the lack of professionalism being shown. She sat down and picked up a copy of a fashion magazine that was lying on the black marble coffee table in front of her. She'd only turned a few pages when a tall, slim woman wearing jeans, a T-shirt and knee-high boots walked in.

'Sorry, Suraj. Damned traffic did me in, and on top of that there's nowhere to park around here,' the woman said, throwing her bags on the floor. 'So are we ready to go? What's the cover shot to be like?'

Suraj threw a glance at Deepa and then replied,

'Well, Prema, it's a simple concept: a steamy set-up between these two.'

Deepa looked up with an anxious glance and Suraj started laughing. Deepa wasn't impressed.

'What's funny?' asked Prema, rummaging hurriedly through her bags, collecting the items she needed for the shoot.

'Oh, just that Miss Deepa Khanna wants to know how "steamy" the shoot is gonna be.'

'Aah, that old chestnut,' said Prema, and she stopped what she was doing for a moment. She looked over at Deepa. 'Darling, if I were you and I was gonna be on the cover of *FilmGlitz* with Ajay Banerjee, I wouldn't be complaining. Enjoy it. We'll do you guys justice.'

'Deepa, are you objecting to getting up close and personal with me?' asked Ajay, with a mock-horrified expression.

'No, no it's fine,' she said, forcing herself to smile.

'Let's get to it then!' enthused Ajay.

Deepa decided she'd better just go with the flow. She was already feeling self-conscious, and by drawing more attention to the matter she was only going to make things worse. So an hour later, following some basic styling, an outfit change and much shouting from Suraj to his staff, Deepa was standing in a clinch with Ajay.

Deepa's body was draped in a white sheet, creating the impression that she was naked underneath, although she was actually wearing a tank top and shorts. Ajay, sporting just a pair of jeans and plenty of oil on his upper body to make his torso shine, had his right arm around Deepa's waist and was staring menacingly into the camera.

Suraj clicked away as hero and heroine threw sultry glances at his lens.

'Deepa honey, I can tell you're conscious of the flesh on show, but just relax,' advised Prema. 'The composition is great. It's not sleazy, trust me. The magazine's gonna be a sell-out.'

Deepa tried to look more comfortable by loosening her shoulders slightly, still making sure she kept a firm grip on the sheet.

'Brilliant!' shouted Suraj. 'That's more like it! Look at him, Deepa. Hold it… Freeze and shoot!'

Deepa kept her gaze on Ajay and finally felt a bit more relaxed, until one of the lighting assistants suddenly yelled, 'Oi, who's that?'

Everyone stopped what they were doing and looked towards the assistant, and then in the direction of the window she was pointing at.

'It's a Peeping Tom!' shouted one of the other

girls. Deepa could see an old man with a short grey beard peering inside.

'Get the hell away from here, dirty old man!' yelled Prema. She reached for the magazine that Deepa had been reading and, rolling it up into a tube, ran towards the window as though she could swat the man away.

His eyes opened wide as he saw Prema running towards him and she was just a couple of feet away when he turned around and darted off. Prema was quite an ordinary-looking woman, but her fake green contact lenses could make her look quite menacing – especially when she was angry. She banged on the glass as the man ran away and then dished out some more abuse.

'Dirty little git, peeping through people's windows and staring at young girls,' she bellowed. 'Shame on you, uncle*ji*!'

Deepa had pulled the white sheet up to cover her bare shoulders.

'You okay?' Ajay asked her over the commotion that had spread throughout the room. Everyone was producing their own theories about who the man could be.

'Yeah, I'm fine,' replied Deepa. 'Was it right to say all that stuff to him though?' she whispered to

Ajay. 'What if he was just looking for someone?'

Ajay pondered. 'He could have had the wrong address, yeah. I guess we shouldn't just assume he's a voyeur. Either way, though, I don't think he'll be back in a hurry.'

'Okay, everyone!' shouted Suraj. 'That's enough discussion. Prema, well done, but can we get back to work now, please? I want to wrap this up. Lights!'

Everyone was a bit more focused this time around. They all wanted to get the job over and done with as soon as possible, especially Deepa. Once Suraj was satisfied that he had enough good shots, Deepa wrapped the sheet tightly around her and rushed to the changing room. She hurriedly put her jeans and white top back on.

'Yes, Amrita, we've just finished,' she shouted into her mobile phone after making her way out of the building. 'Boy, am I glad that shoot is out of the way! It was really awkward. Eventful too, though – I'll tell you about it later. I'll meet you at India TV,' she added. 'Just go straight to Mike Malik's studio. I'll see you in the dressing rooms.'

'Oooh, who's appearing on *India Tonight*?' came Ajay's voice from behind. He had been standing outside the building too. 'Wouldn't be Deepa Khanna the Superstar by any chance?'

'Not quite in your league yet, Mr Banerjee,' Deepa said in jest. 'But showing my face on these channels means I get a better chance to claw my way up to where you are.'

'Well, in my books you're already up there,' he quipped. 'You're head and shoulders above the competition, missy.'

'Thanks, Ajay. It's kind of you to say so,' said Deepa, flattered.

'I mean it, I really do.'

Deepa smiled at him. She wasn't certain whether he really did mean what he said but it felt good to hear it all the same. She looked up and saw her driver pulling up. 'My cab's here, do you need to go anywhere?'

'How about your house?'

Deepa laughed. 'No, seriously, I mean do you need a lift?'

'If you're the one picking me up, sure.'

'You know what I mean, Ajay,' said Deepa, walking over to the car and opening the back door.

'I'm fine thanks, sweetie. My dad's coming to get me, actually. We've got dinner round my grandma's tonight – every Friday night without fail or we're dead meat.'

'Aaah, that's so sweet. You're so lucky to have

grandparents,' said Deepa. 'I've only got one grandmother – my *naani* – but I never met either of my grandfathers.'

'Well… there is a way my granddad can become your granddad,' he proposed. 'Mull it over.'

'You're impossible!' she laughed as she shut the door of the taxi.

As it pulled away, she looked at Ajay in the rear-view mirror. She could see he was still smiling and watching as the car drove off into the distance. It was as though he didn't want to let her out of his sight. Deepa's heart skipped a beat.

Maybe, just maybe, she and Ajay were destined to be more than just co-stars.

* * *

'Right, Amrita, if you can just sort my hair out again then you can go home – unless you want to stay with me until the end of the programme.' Deepa had arrived at the India TV recording studio and she took the sparkly blue slide out of her hair so Amrita could get on with transforming her.

'I'd love to, but no can do, honey. I've got another shoot really early tomorrow, and I need to go home and get some rest.'

'Fair enough,' said Deepa. 'So, come on then,

what are you gonna do with my hair now?'

'Well,' said Amrita, moving around so she could see Deepa's face from different angles. 'You've had the straight-hair look for the day, perhaps we can go for a glamorous evening style now. What about a 1960s-style bouffant look? Think Brigitte Bardot.'

'Like a beehive?'

'You got it,' replied Amrita.

'Why Bardot?' asked Deepa. 'All our actresses had them too – even my *naani* was a fan! Some of the pictures she's got from when she was a young woman are amazing. She has this cute little white bun now, but back then she used to have this huge, amazing hairstyle – every day of the week!'

'Yeah, my gran used to do that too. She called it a 'puff bun' or something like that. Actually, you're so popular right now you could wear it a few times and it would make a comeback.'

'I love that idea, Amrita!' said Deepa, clapping her hands with glee.

Just then, one of the researchers from the chat show entered the room holding a notepad and pen. 'Hello, Madam,' whispered the young girl nervously.

'Call me Deepa,' smiled the actress. 'You must be about the same age as me, right? Calling me Madam makes me sound twenty years older!'

The researcher smiled awkwardly to reveal a pearly white set of teeth that were being strangled by silver braces. 'Come this way Madam… urrghh… Deepa Miss,' she stumbled. 'I'll show you the studio.'

'Deepa Miss? 'I like it!' laughed Deepa. 'What's your name?'

'Pooja.'

'Right – Pooja Miss! Let's go.'

Both girls giggled and it wasn't long before Pooja was bouncing happily alongside Deepa as they walked together to the studio.

When they got there, Deepa looked up at a big sign above the door. It said 'LIVE ON AIR'.

'That'll light up when the programme goes out,' said Pooja, smiling.

Deepa gulped. 'That's made me feel really nervous. I've got proper butterflies in my stomach now,' she said, taking a deep breath in.

'Are you all right, Deepa Miss?' asked Pooja, looking concerned.

'I've never been on live television before – what if I mess it up? How many thousands of people are going to be watching this?'

'You won't mess up… I'm sure of it,' replied Pooja. She looked admiringly at Deepa and then chuckled. 'You're a famous film star… you're so beautiful… so nice… how can you be scared of TV?'

'Well, we can have as many takes as we want for films,' said Deepa candidly. 'But this is once and once only. Mess up and you've made a right idiot of yourself.'

'You'll be fine,' smiled Pooja as she led Deepa through the door. Deepa didn't know what to expect, and she looked keenly around the simple set. There was very little furniture – just two black seats under a blue spotlight and a small round table with two glasses of water neatly placed on silver coasters.

Pooja pointed to where Deepa would be sitting. 'I'll bring you back in forty minutes. Mike will be here in half an hour.'

Deepa nodded and then made her way back to the dressing room to let Amrita create the beehive they'd discussed. She settled back in the chair and closed her eyes to relax as Amrita began sectioning her hair and backcombing. She then applied thick, '60s-style eyeliner to the top of Deepa's eyelids. In just thirty minutes, the young stylist had transformed Deepa from modern starlet to classic beauty.

'Oh my God!' exclaimed Deepa looking in the mirror. 'I don't even recognise myself. I look amazing, but more like twenty five than seventeen!'

'Well, that is the idea,' replied Amrita. 'You don't

want people to see you as a newcomer any more… this look says established star.'

Deepa stared in disbelief at the stunning woman looking back at her from the mirror. She may have been reluctant to join the movies, but she was definitely taking to it.

As she walked back into the studio, she was suddenly blooming with confidence. Even the LIVE ON AIR sign glowing brightly above the door didn't daunt her.

'So, Deepa,' began Mike once she was seated in front of him. 'A bit of a rags-to-riches fairy tale for you, isn't it?'

'Well, I wouldn't quite say rags, Mike, but we were definitely not rich. And then my first two films didn't do that well so I wasn't at all sure of my future in the business,' Deepa said frankly. 'But I'm getting lots of good offers now, so I hope to be around for a few years. If,' she added, looking around at the audience, 'these guys still want me.'

The crowd cheered loudly to show they did indeed want her around, and Deepa raised her arms above her head and clapped as a show of appreciation.

'I've heard you never actually set out to be a star, Deepa. That it was your parents who pushed you into the business. True?'

Deepa's smile briefly left her face. This wasn't a question she had anticipated. 'Well, it wasn't a childhood dream of mine, but my dad always felt I had the talent needed to succeed here. I guess he saw the potential I didn't,' she responded cleverly. 'My mum was never pushy. She always said I should do whatever I wanted to, but, yeah, my dad was keen for me to pursue films. He never got to sing and dance around trees himself, perhaps he's living out his desires through my work!'

The audience laughed and Deepa smiled back, relieved to have got herself out of a tight spot. Fortunately, the questions that followed were more straightforward. Mike obviously found her very easy on the eye and was content just to flirt with her for the rest of the interview.

'Ladies and gentlemen, let's hear it for the dazzling Deepa!' he said at the end.

Another round of applause followed. The superstar and chat show host sat talking while the lights shining down on them dimmed, bringing the show to a close.

As the audience started making its way out of the studio, the bright studio lights came back on again.

'Okay guys, we're done,' said the producer, removing his headphones. 'Great show, thanks

Deepa. I think viewers will really have enjoyed that.'

'No problem,' she replied as she got up off her chair. 'I enjoyed it too.'

Deepa raised a hand to her beehive to make sure it was all still in place, and then took her mobile out of her bag and dialled her driver's number. Pooja rushed back into the studio, ready to show Deepa out, but waited patiently behind the actress once she saw she was making a call.

'Yes, I'll meet you outside,' Deepa confirmed. As she spoke, she looked out into the rows of empty seats that just a few minutes earlier had been packed with people. Her eyes stopped at one seat that hadn't been vacated yet. Deepa squinted at the only person left in the auditorium.

She gasped.

Although she had caught only a glimpse of him through a half-open window, Deepa was certain this was the same 'Peeping Tom' who had been at the photo studio earlier in the day.

'How about a drink in the bar, Deepa?'

Deepa was startled. It was Mike, the TV show host, standing right behind her.

'Gosh, you're jumpy,' he said. 'Anything wrong?'

'Urrgh… no… no,' replied Deepa. 'I didn't know you were there, that's all.'

'Sorry, didn't mean to scare you. Just wanted to know if you're free to have a quick drink,' he said, winking. 'I could do with one, it's been a long day.'

'I'd love to, Mike, but my driver's gonna be outside in a few minutes and I have a really early start tomorrow. Some other time?'

'I'll hold you to that,' said Mike, pulling a business card from his back trouser pocket. He caught hold of Deepa's hand and placed the card firmly on her palm. In no hurry to let go, he leaned towards her and whispered, 'Call me.'

'Yeah… will do. See you Mike,' Deepa laughed nervously. She wriggled around and finally managed to free her hand.

By now, Deepa was very eager to leave. She gestured to Pooja that she was ready to go and as the girls walked towards the exit door, Deepa's heart pounded and her hands felt clammy. She plucked up her courage and stole a glance back at the seats in the studio. Deepa wasn't sure whether she should be very relieved or very afraid.

The mystery man had disappeared again.

Chapter 3

'Yeah, why don't we then?' she asked as she tossed her head back on to her bed. It was gone midnight and Deepa was still up, chatting on the phone.

'I'd love to see you now, how about it?'

'What?' asked Deepa in disbelief. 'At this time of night? You must be crazy!'

'Crazy for you, you mean. Yep, I sure am. I'll wait for you by the Clock Tower on Pall Road. Half an hour?'

'Oh my God! How can I possibly get out at this time of night?' she asked. 'My parents will never let me go. Plus I've got an early start in the morning.'

'Who asked you to tell your parents?' came the reply. 'I'm not telling mine. I want to see you now. My driver will be outside your house in ten to fifteen minutes. See you in a bit. Can't wait… bye.'

The phone went dead.

Deepa jumped up. She felt dizzy with excitement at the thought of a late-night rendezvous with Ajay Banerjee and also at the thrill of doing something so rebellious. She stopped to think for a moment before tip-toeing out of her bedroom. She went down the hall and slowly turned the handle of Sachin's bedroom door.

'Sachin… Sach…'

A loud groan emanated from beneath the duvet.

'Sachin! *Psst!* Get up! I need your help.'

'Huh?' Sachin peered over the top of his duvet, barely able to open his eyes. 'What do you want?'

'Shhh! Keep your voice down. I need to go out for a couple of hours and I want you to keep a lookout for me,' Deepa whispered in his ear. 'If

Mum or Dad get up and you think they're gonna go in my room – which I doubt they will – can you just distract them, or something? Worst-case scenario, tell them there was a last-minute dubbing call for me and I had to go.'

'But where are you going? And who with?' asked Sachin, annoyed that Deepa had disrupted his sleep, but also concerned because she didn't have a habit of creeping out in the dead of the night.

'Now's not the time,' she said. 'I'll tell you tomorrow. But call me if there's serious trouble.'

'Hmm.' He slid back under the covers and turned over.

Deepa crept back into her bedroom and then stood with her hands clasped together as she worked out what to wear. It was a warm, humid evening in Mumbai so she grabbed a strappy, full-length summer dress from her wardrobe and hurriedly threw it on along with a pair of ankle-strap heels. Very quietly, she shut the bedroom door behind her and, pursing her lips tightly, tiptoed down the stairs.

Sure enough, as Ajay had promised, a car was standing outside the Khanna family's residence.

Nervous, and with half a mind to turn around and run back inside, Deepa climbed into the back seat of the vehicle after confirming the driver had been sent by Ajay. As it set off, the driver peered into his rear-view mirror to get a good look at his famous passenger. 'I liked *Mumbai Magic*, good songs. Very big star now, hey?' he smiled, revealing two gold teeth.

Deepa felt embarrassed at being recognised while creeping out after dark for a date and was suddenly worried about who else might find out about this. 'Yes, well, it took a while but we got there in the end,' she said simply.

To avoid catching his eye and inviting any more questions, Deepa stared out of the window for the rest of the journey, and as soon as the car stopped by Pall Road's Clock Tower she rushed to get out.

Biting her nails nervously as she waited, Deepa looked around at people walking past, but quickly turned away if anyone looked in her direction. She was beginning to wish she'd stayed at home, but then a car drew up and a figure emerged. As soon as she caught sight of Ajay, all her doubts vanished. He was dressed in a smart blue shirt and black trousers and looked very slick. Deepa couldn't help but smile.

'Hey, Deepa,' he said cheerfully as he leaned forward to give her a peck on the cheek. 'So glad you could make it. I did wonder whether you'd actually turn up.'

'I must be mad, sneaking out in the middle of the night, but I didn't want to disappoint you,' she said, flicking her hair away from her face.

Ajay then walked over to the driver and whispered something to him. The driver turned to look at Deepa and then grinned before setting off.

'What did you say?' Deepa asked Ajay. 'Was it about me? He seems a bit weird… do you trust him? I don't want this leaking out in the magazines, it's really important.'

'Don't worry,' said Ajay. 'You actresses worry way too much. He's been with me for ten years, he's fine. I told him to be on standby so he can take you back home, that's all.'

Deepa relaxed and Ajay gently took her hand in his. Her heart started thumping wildly, but she tried to keep a cool exterior. The pair strolled down to the beachfront and spent the next few hours sitting on a bench facing the sea. They chatted away about their families, film careers and the future.

Both Deepa and Ajay had grown up in ordinary, middle-class households and it was quite rare for those with no connections to the film industry to even get a break, let alone make it big.

Time flew past as Deepa shared with Ajay some of the difficulties she faced as she adapted to her newfound fame and status as a star. It was only when her phone rang that she realised what time it was.

'You'd better get back here fast!' ordered Sachin. 'Dad's up already, it's nearly four o'clock – time for his prayers. He hasn't gone into your room, but he knows you've got an early start so he might. Don't make me lie *Didi*, come back quick!'

'Okay, Sachin, okay,' replied Deepa, feeling slightly panicky again. 'I'll be as quick as I can.'

Ajay made a call to his driver as soon as Deepa told him she wanted to go, and then tenderly took her hand again, leading her back up the narrow street to where the car would pull up. As soon as the driver arrived, Deepa pulled her hand back.

'You think he reckons we had a business meeting or something?' whispered Ajay in Deepa's ear. 'He knows what's going on here.'

'I know,' said Deepa, biting her lip. 'But I still feel awkward holding hands with you in front of him. He's my dad's age – it's embarrassing.'

'Aah, that's what I love about you, Deepa Khanna. Such a conservative, middle-class girl at heart!'

Deepa laughed and as Ajay took a few steps towards her and leaned forward, her heart fluttered. She had never dated seriously before but here she was, in a clinch with Ajay Banerjee. Gazing into his sensual brown eyes and able to feel his warm breath on her face, she couldn't believe her luck. Her idol was to be the first person she would kiss.

* * *

'Ajay's amazing!' drooled Deepa to fellow starlet, Bela. 'He's so gentle and so considerate… he sent a car to pick me up and we chatted all night on the beach, it was really romantic.'

The girls sat together as they waited to start shooting a song for a film starring some unknown newcomers. It was a low-budget production and two songs featuring high-profile stars were being added to the movie to give it more commercial value. Deepa and Bela were to appear in one of them.

'He's a nice guy, I hope it works out for you,' smiled Bela. 'How do you get time for romance though? I hardly have a chance to breathe!'

'Well, movies and money aren't everything, after all. I want to have some fun or there's no point in being in this business.'

'Yeah, guess you're right.'

'And there's plenty of time to get serious about work,' mused Deepa. 'Right now, I'm having a better time with Ajay behind the scenes than in front of the cameras.'

'Fair enough,' said Bela, holding her hand up to signal to the director, Sukh Singh, that she had seen him. 'We're ready to go.'

'I forgot to ask,' said Bela as the girls walked towards the set. 'Fancy coming to a party tonight? It's the opening of a restaurant and I could do with some company.'

Deepa shook her head. 'I'd like to, but I might be meeting Ajay again tonight. Sorry.'

'No worries. You have fun. I'm sure the party will be really boring, but I have to go as the restaurant is owned by one of my producers. My friends are busy, so I've got to go on my own.'

'You girls ready?' shouted Sukh Singh. They nodded. 'You look fabulous, both of you,' he complimented. 'Nicely coordinated.'

They were both wearing plain-coloured sarees, Deepa was in blue with pink jewellery and shoes while Bela wore pink with blue accessories. The song they were due to shoot was a dream sequence in which the hero of the film, played by debut actor Johnny Jaffrey, was to imagine himself in the company of two famous actresses, so the girls were playing themselves.

Johnny was standing a few feet away, rehearsing his steps with the male choreographer, Mithun. He looked completely star-struck when he was introduced to Bela and Deepa.

'So nice to meet you,' Bela greeted him, as professional as ever. She held her hand out for Johnny to shake and he complied, but no words came out of his mouth. He just stood there, grinning and nodding but utterly tongue-tied. When Deepa smiled at him and mouthed 'hi', he just grinned at her too.

'He's the son of a producer,' whispered Bela to Deepa when Johnny had turned away. 'Nobody knows him yet but his dad's spending a fortune on his launch.'

'Oh! That explains it,' replied Deepa, also in a hushed tone. 'He'd never have got the break otherwise. He's not exactly eye candy, is he?'

Both girls started giggling but were quickly interrupted by the choreographer. 'Ready to dance?' asked Mithun.

The starlets nodded keenly and Mithun proceeded to show them their steps. Bela picked them up instantly, but for Deepa it was a different story.

'Come on, Deepa,' urged Mithun as he went through the sequence for the third time. 'It's easy, you know… Bela's managed it.'

'Sorry sir,' Deepa apologised. 'I'll try again.'

The music came on and Bela and Deepa stood ready for the cue to start dancing. Both girls had to perform a series of small steps, followed by a twirl. They each had to rush towards Johnny and put their heads on his shoulders at exactly the same moment.

Bela got into her stride straight away, proving what an expert she really was. She completed the sequence easily and with great expression. Deepa managed the first step but then got her footwork wrong, which meant her timing for the twirl was completely out. By the time she had to run towards Johnny, she was flustered and so behind that she literally had to chase Bela to get to him on time.

'Cut! Cut! Cut!' shouted Sukh Singh. 'That was awful. Deepa – really bad! You look as though you're running after Bela rather than towards Johnny!'

'Sukh's right, Deepa,' said Mithun. 'Where's the grace and poise? You might be able to get away with that if it was just you on your own, but next to Bela, you really show yourself up.'

Deepa felt humiliated. She looked around and saw some of the unit members watching in silence. One of the younger spot boys was laughing, although he tried to stop himself when Deepa's gaze fell upon him. He looked down at the floor, but carried on sniggering.

'Give us five minutes,' Bela urged Sukh. 'We'll have another practice, she'll be fine.'

'I'm off to make a few calls. I'll be in the café next door,' Sukh said, obviously annoyed. 'Call me on my mobile when you're ready,' he told Mithun.

'Sure,' said Mithun. 'Right, focus this time. Music please!' he called.

Once the music began, he first did a run-through of the steps himself and then asked Deepa to have a go on her own.

'I'll try,' she said, hoping nobody would realise that dancing didn't come very naturally to her.

Deepa started off really well, but again she faltered at the turn. Mithun shook his head.

'What's wrong with you, Deepa? It's so simple. Even the new hero has managed better than you. Do it again.'

'Sorry, Mithun*ji*. I'm really tired, I had a restless night, so my brain's feeling fuzzy.'

Bela looked at Deepa as it dawned on her what had happened. Deepa's night out with Ajay had meant she didn't get enough sleep and was now finding it hard to concentrate.

Finally though, after two more attempts, Deepa

did manage to get the sequence into her head, and once Mithun was confident she wouldn't cause any more delays he called the director back.

'Right, are we ready now?' asked Sukh as he stomped back on to the set. He was looking straight at Deepa.

'Yes, we are,' she said meekly, anxious for the music to start so she could prove it. Following the cue from Mithun, the song began and the two girls danced, twirled and then ran to their waiting hero. Both were smiling broadly as they rested their heads against Johnny's shoulders, Deepa on the left and Bela on the right.

'Cut! That was okay… and about time too,' said Sukh bluntly. 'Now for sequence two.'

Deepa had to concentrate extra hard to make sure she kept on top of things and was very relieved, and very tired, when four hours later, Sukh announced that they were done for the day.

Deepa rushed into the make-up room and hurriedly took her mobile out of her bag. Four missed calls from Ajay! Deepa was delighted and quickly dialled his number. The call went to voicemail.

'Hi, this is Ajay speaking. Kindly leave a message and I'll get back to you as soon as I can.'

'Hi Ajay… Deepa here. Sorry I missed your calls. Had a disastrous day at the office… ummm… ummm… talk to you tonight, maybe? Ciao.'

Deepa hung up and then cringed to herself about the message she'd just left. Why 'ciao'? It definitely wasn't something she'd normally say. She'd been trying to come across as sophisticated and cool, but as she replayed the message in her head she was sure she'd just sounded really corny.

Deepa unwrapped her saree, folding it as best she could, and hung it up on the clothes rail before slipping into a denim skirt and a T-shirt. She left the dressing room and shut the door behind her. When she reached the exit gate of the studio she saw her mum in the back seat of the taxi.

It was a nice surprise. After the incident at Javed's Audio Visual Cave, Deepa had spent an hour trying to convince her mum that the boy who claimed he'd been dating her was either mistaken or mad. Her mum had finally accepted her word and they were on good terms again.

As Deepa settled in and they set off on their way, Ajay sent her a text message. 'Who's that?' asked Shanta, peering over at her daughter's phone.

'Just a friend,' she replied, eagerly opening it but being careful to shield its contents from her mum.

'Hi babe. Meet again tonight? Same time, same place? AJ'

'Yes! Deepa X'

She smiled away to herself. The difficulties she'd endured on the set didn't matter much any more. As she had told Bela, to her, matters of the heart were far more important.

* * *

'I heard you couldn't dance today. What went wrong?' Deepa's dad didn't even wait until she got through the door and Deepa was stunned. How could he have heard about this already?

'All this money I've spent on you, it's not going to waste, okay? Do you understand me, Deepa?' he scolded. 'Your career was nearly finished before it even started, so thank God for *Mumbai Magic*. It was a lifeline. But if you mess up now, I'll marry you off to the highest bidder, mark my words.'

Then he stormed back into the sitting room, slamming the door behind him.

Deepa came down to earth with a thud. She went off to her bedroom and shut the door behind her. Shanta scurried after her.

'*Beti*, don't take it to heart,' came Shanta's soft, gentle voice from the other side of the bedroom door. 'Your dad doesn't know how to communicate… you know what he's like.'

Deepa sat down on her bed and closed her eyes. They had been over this all before, time and time again, and Deepa just didn't want to hear it any more. It wasn't her mum's fault, though, and she mustered up the emotional strength to say a few words. 'Don't worry, mum. I'm fine, just tired. I think I'll have a rest. I'll be down later.'

After a few moments, she heard her mother's footsteps going back downstairs. Deepa couldn't be bothered to change. She crawled into her bed and closed her weary eyes.

She hated the way her father made her feel and she hated herself for allowing him to get to her. Try as she might, she wasn't able to just shrug it off.

Deepa felt she had done incredibly well to get a foothold in the industry considering she had no contacts or godfathers to give her a leg up. But she also knew that nothing short of mega-stardom was ever going to be good enough for her dad. She felt destined always to be a failure in his eyes.

Tears streamed down her cheeks. The weight of the emotion she was feeling combined with the weight of her eyelids meant it wasn't long before she was fast asleep.

Chapter 4

'What rubbish! She was here all night. She's here now, right behind me. If it was some other starlet I may well believe it… but not my Deepa! She lives in my house and I know she'd never do a thing like that. If you choose to believe everything some idiot tells you, that's your problem Patil *sahib*.'

Deepa's dad slammed the phone down. 'Bloody fool! That was Patil from *The Weekly Star*,' he said, turning to look at Deepa. She had peered into the room to see what had upset her father so early in the morning. 'Wants to know who you were out with last night.'

'What?' she asked. 'I was home.'

'I know! That bloody Patil, I've only met him a few times and now he's making out he's a family friend. But all he really wants is gossip. You can't trust anyone these days!'

Jayant brushed past her and then ranted all the way up the stairs, slamming the bathroom door behind him. Deepa stood lost in thought, drumming her fingers on her lips. She didn't know quite what to make of it all, but she was determined to find out more.

'Amrita, you haven't heard anything about me have you? Some story about me going out last night with somebody,' she asked over the phone.

'No, why?'

'A reporter called my dad this morning and said something about me being out with someone, I assume they were talking about a guy. Thing is, I was out the night before with Ajay… I'm worried someone's got wind of that.'

'Oh, I say! Well, if you're gonna get up to mischief, that's what'll happen,' laughed Amrita. 'Why didn't you tell me about going out with Ajay? What happened? Where did you go? I want all the details!'

'Not a good time now,' whispered Deepa. 'I'll fill you in later. My dad'll go nuts if he finds out I was with him. You know how he wants me to focus on my career and nothing else.'

'Yeah, we all know that!'

'Second problem is I might be in the dog house with Ajay too,' Deepa revealed.

'Oh?'

'I was supposed to go out with him again last night but ended up falling asleep. My phone was on silent and the next thing I know, it's five in the morning. I had loads of missed calls… he'd been waiting for me by Pall Road.'

'You stood him up?' asked Amrita, aghast. 'OH MY GOD! You can't do that to a superstar like Ajay! Is he still talking to you?'

'Just about. I had to really grovel on the phone just now. He's agreed to meet me for lunch today, after a script hearing I have to go to.'

'Oh dear… it's all happening to you, isn't it babe?'

sympathised Amrita. 'Don't stress, okay? Ajay will understand and I'm sure your dad won't find out. Just say it's gossip… that's what everyone else does!'

'Yeah, guess I'll have to. We'll see, got to go now. Okay Amrita, I'll catch you up later,' Deepa finished, grabbing her handbag and keys and rushing out of the door.

She spent the next two hours at the house of producer Steve Sethi, where they read through the script for a big budget movie. Deepa accepted the part on the spot – not only did she fall in love with her role of a petty thief, but Ajay Banerjee was to be cast opposite her as well. Talk about mixing business with pleasure, she thought to herself as Steve went through the schedule with her.

By the time Deepa left Steve's house, she was running ten minutes late, so she tried to contact Ajay on his mobile to let him know. She was also bursting to tell him the exciting news about them working together on this latest assignment but Ajay's phone rang a couple of times and then the line went dead. Deepa was puzzled. It was almost as though Ajay had hung up on her, although she was sure he wouldn't do that.

Feeling slightly hassled now and not being helped by her high heels, Deepa ran awkwardly towards the side street where her taxi was waiting. 'Pall Road, Clock Tower,' she puffed. All of a sudden, she was very hot and bothered, and as she looked at herself in the small vanity mirror she kept in her handbag she saw beads of sweat on her brow.

Deepa grabbed a tissue and dabbed her forehead. Then she got some powder out of her handbag and applied it carefully. She added a slick of lip gloss, ran a comb through her hair and by the time her taxi had reached her destination, she was looking pristine again.

There were quite a few people about in this plush part of Mumbai but Deepa spotted Ajay immediately. He was sitting on one of the stone steps at the foot of the Clock Tower. He was wearing his sunglasses and looked very cool. Deepa's heart raced as she imagined walking along the beach hand-in-hand with him again. She put on a large sunhat to avoid being recognised, stepped out of the car and rushed to meet him.

'Hey Ajay, sorry I'm late,' she apologised. 'I tried to call you. The narration for Steve Sethi's movie took a lot longer than I thought it would, but it's such a great script, isn't it?'

Ajay sat there in silence. His head was turned away from Deepa and he seemed to be staring blankly into the distance.

'What's wrong? Has something happened?'

Ajay sighed. He looked down and shook his head.

'What? What's wrong? Tell me,' urged Deepa. She was feeling anxious now. 'Is it to do with the film? Did Steve Sethi call you? He told me it was mine if I wanted it. I said "yes".'

'It's NOT the film,' said Ajay sharply, finally looking up at her. 'I just don't like it when people play games with me.'

'Huh?' she said.

'Don't play dumb – you know what I mean!'

Deepa shifted her feet nervously. She moved a couple of steps closer to him, conscious of the fact that passers-by may be able to hear them.

'We've only met once,' Ajay went on, removing his shades and looking Deepa in the eye. 'I don't understand why you feel the need to lie to me or make out you're something you're not.'

She stared at him, clutching the shoulder strap of her handbag with both hands. She was half expecting him to suddenly burst out laughing and say that this was all just a joke. There was no such response.

Head down again, Ajay told her: 'It's not like you're tied to me or anything. I don't get why you couldn't be honest with me last night. If you had plans or you want to play the field, just say so.'

'What? I've never lied to you!' exclaimed Deepa, raising a hand to her mouth in shock. 'I told you – I fell asleep. I was at home and my phone was on silent… I had such a bad day yesterday, my song shoot went wrong… it was awful. And then my dad started on me as soon as I walked through the door. I only planned to sleep for a bit, but when I got up, it was five o'clock. I'm really sorry.'

Ajay leapt up so fast, he made Deepa jump back. '*This* is what I'm talking about, Deepa!' he said, raising his voice. He had his sunglasses in his hand and was pointing them at her. 'We're not exactly an item, so why make up stories? Be yourself! I know you were out last night – Bela told me.'

'What? Bela?' asked Deepa, totally confused. 'Why would she tell you I was out last night? She must have been talking about the daytime. We were shooting together yesterday… that's when I messed up the dance sequence.'

'Yes, I heard about that too and she told me that she invited you to an event last night. You told her you couldn't make it, but then you turned up really late anyway – and you were with some other guy.'

Deepa dropped her handbag to the floor and

stood with her hands on her hips. This was unbelievable.

'Don't mess with me, Deepa. I get the message – you're not into a serious thing here, that's fine.'

'Look, this is crazy! I don't know how to convince you,' said Deepa, with her hands in the air. 'Why would Bela tell you something like that? It's not true!'

'Bela's a good friend of mine. We've worked together before and she's obviously looking out for me,' Ajay responded, springing to his friend's defence. 'She said you'd told her we met up the night before. That's why she couldn't believe you were being so blatant with someone else at the party. Were you drunk or something?' he asked bluntly. 'Because Bela said she tried to talk to you but you just laughed at her and walked off.'

Deepa stood listening, hardly able to make sense of what she was hearing. She slumped down on to the stone step, not knowing whether to laugh or cry. She was silent for a few moments, realising that Ajay wasn't going to believe her whatever she said. He had already made up his mind. Still, she was desperate to try and make him see sense – she had one more go.

'Look Ajay, forget Bela… I don't know why she'd

want to make up something as nasty as that. She either wants you for herself or she just thought she saw me – maybe it was my double,' said Deepa, aware she was clutching at straws. 'Or maybe it was Bela who was drunk, and she confused somebody else for me.'

'Come on, Deepa,' said Ajay firmly. 'Stop digging a deeper hole for yourself. If you'd just been straight with me in the beginning and said you wanted to keep things casual, I would have been disappointed, but I'd have understood. Now I just feel like you're making a fool of me.'

Ajay put his shades on again and walked away.

'Where are you going, Ajay?' cried Deepa, running after him. She grabbed his arm, but he shrugged his shoulder and continued towards his waiting car.

'No hard feelings. See you around,' he said as he jumped in. He didn't turn around to look at her again. Within a few seconds, the car had sped off, kicking up some Mumbai dust as it headed away.

Deepa stood rooted to the spot, not quite believing what had just happened. Standing on Pall Road on her own, she felt helpless and heartbroken. She took a few steps back to the Clock Tower and sat down on the step.

She thought long and hard about what Ajay had said and it started to dawn on her that there were similarities between the story she'd just heard and the phone call her father had received that morning. Patil the reporter must have got his information from the same source – Bela. But why would Bela spread such malicious gossip? Was it really so she could get in there with Ajay? Deepa knew there was only one way to find out.

She hailed a cab.

'Raj Chopra Studios, please,' she said to the taxi driver. Deepa's mind was full of anguish and she almost didn't hear her phone bleeping insistently inside her bag. She grabbed the phone, hoping it might be Ajay, but was disappointed to see her dad's name flash up on the display. She sighed and pressed the button to take the call. 'I got the part Dad, I'll talk to you later. I'm having my legs waxed.'

'Oh… oh… oh, okay speak to you later.'

Deepa's brain was whirring as she tried to process all the emotions she was feeling. She was devastated that Ajay didn't believe her story, but she was also mad at herself for falling asleep the night before and failing to meet him. And she was *furious* with Bela.

'Wait right here, don't move!' Deepa ordered the taxi driver as he pulled up outside the studio, alongside an ice cream cart.

'Ice cream *lelo memsahib*,' urged the dishevelled street vendor, holding the *kulfi* on a stick up close to her face.

'No!' yelled Deepa. 'I don't want your bloody ice cream!'

Taken aback, he stood and stared at her as she rushed off to talk to the security guard outside the studio gates.

'Is Bela in the West part of the studio or South?' Deepa asked a worker once she had been let through. Deepa knew Bela was shooting here for the whole week as she recalled her talking to somebody about it when they'd been filming together.

'South,' he replied, smiling and looking Deepa up and down.

Without even bothering to thank him and in spite of her killer heels, Deepa ran as fast as she could until she reached the part of the studio known as the South Wing.

She peered in through a glass door and saw Bela sitting, heavily dressed up, with a cup of tea in her hand. Deepa opened the door and walked towards her, telling herself to stay as calm as possible.

'I need to talk to you Bela. Come outside now,' Deepa ordered.

'Sure,' said Bela, a bit surprised. She handed her tea to her make-up man, giving him a cursory glance, and then followed Deepa outside.

'You okay?' asked Bela. 'You look really distressed.'

'Okay? No. Distressed? Yes I am. Thanks to you.' Deepa stood with her arms folded tightly across her chest.

'Sorry?'

'You better be sorry,' Deepa spat out. 'Making up stories about me and ruining my chances with Ajay. What's your problem? Do you want him for yourself, is that it?'

'*Whoa, whoa!*' said Bela, moving backwards, reeling from the force of Deepa's accusation. 'What stories? I haven't made up any stories.'

'I was at home all last night,' insisted Deepa. 'But somebody's been telling lies about me... saying I was at some party with a guy who is NOT Ajay.'

'I wasn't lying,' said Bela. 'I mentioned it to Ajay because I happened to be chatting to him this morning and he was telling me he's really serious about you.'

'Oh really? So you thought you'd get in there and mess it up for me?' shouted Deepa.

Hearing Deepa raise her voice, Bela's make-up man, Micky, came bursting through the door.

'What's up, Bela?'

'Nothing, Micky. It's fine,' said Bela.

'Apart from you trying to ruin my life, you mean!' yelled Deepa. Her effort to contain her emotions was failing miserably.

'I don't understand what's going on,' Bela remarked to Micky. 'I saw Deepa last night at a party and now she says she was in all night... that it wasn't her.'

'Too damn right it wasn't me! Can you prove I was there?'

'Well, no…'

'Exactly!

'Hang on, girls,' said Micky, trying to calm things down. It was no good though, Deepa was on the warpath.

'You'd better stop meddling in my affairs,' she raged, pointing her finger. 'When you make up these lies, it's not just Ajay you turn against me, a reporter called my dad this morning to ask about my so-called night out with a strange man. I don't take things like that lightly!'

'But Dee–'

'Don't Deepa me, don't pretend you're my friend… Just go and find your own man!' she hissed, turning on her heel and stomping off in anger.

Deepa didn't turn to look around and, without thinking about what she was doing, she started running down the corridor towards the exit gate. Now that she had vented her anger, the pain and hurt began to overwhelm her. Deepa was heartbroken. She may well have lost Ajay for good.

All around, people working in the studio stopped what they were doing and stared at Deepa as she ran, tears streaming down her pretty face. She got to the gate and lifted her hand, indicating to the security guard to let her out. The man with the brown turban and big beard didn't say a word, but Deepa saw that he was sympathetic. He handed her a tissue as she walked out. Again, she failed to say "thank you". She wanted to, but no words came out.

Deepa saw her waiting taxi, opened the door and sat down. She then put her head in her hands and sobbed loudly all the way home.

* * *

If Deepa thought things couldn't get much worse than they had, she was wrong. Although she'd intended to remain calm when confronting Bela, she hadn't. She drew so much attention to herself at Raj Chopra Studios that tongues were wagging long after she had gone.

And now, wanting to know exactly what had transpired, reporters had been camped outside the Khanna residence since the early hours.

'Deepa Khanna! Deepa Khanna!' cried one eager journalist as she left the house with her mother. He was carrying a huge microphone with 'STAR BUZZ RADIO' emblazoned on it. 'What happened at Raj Chopra Studios yesterday? Can you confirm or deny that you and Bela were fighting over Ajay Banerjee?'

Deepa didn't dare look his way. It was evident she was stressed, but she kept her head down. 'Mum, ignore them; don't say a word, okay?' She ushered Shanta towards the car.

Shanta looked annoyed but did as she was told. Jayant, however, wasn't so compliant. He'd already had a go at Deepa for being so indiscreet in confronting Bela, and now he turned his wrath on the reporters.

'Get the hell out of here, you scumbags!' he shouted as he opened the front door and ran outside. 'Before I call the police! Out, out!' he yelled, picking up a cricket bat that was lying on the marble tiles by the gate of his residence. He began swinging wildly, and within seconds all the reporters had moved back and Deepa's car was able to get on its way to a radio station where Deepa was to be interviewed.

'Okay, so you won't tell them, but you can let me know what all this craziness is about!' Shanta said once they were safely out of view. 'First that weird incident in the record shop and now people are saying they've seen you with yet another man. And what's all this about Ajay? Are you sure you haven't been messing around, Deepa? Please tell me. I need to know,' she pleaded. 'I can't defend you unless I'm one hundred per cent certain of what you're up to.'

Deepa looked at her mum through her huge pink shades and lowered her head. She sighed and then grabbed hold of her mother's hand. 'It's not what you think, Mum,' she said calmly. 'I haven't been dating anybody – especially not that guy in the record shop. We've been through that already.'

'Is there some *chakkar* with somebody else?'

'Not exactly.'

'Well, is there something brewing then? Do we know him? Is it Ajay? Is that why the reporters keep mentioning his name?'

Deepa stayed quiet.

'Be honest with me, Deepa. This is bad enough for us all as it is – reporters outside our house day and night. I need to know what's happening!'

Deepa let go of Shanta's hand and looked out of the window. It was painful for her to admit that there was nothing going on with Ajay, but it was the truth. 'It's nothing, Mum, I just got chatting to Ajay the other day at the photo shoot... I've only seen him a handful of times in my whole life and it's always been work-related, although I do think he likes me.'

'And you?' Shanta stared intently at her daughter. It was as though she could read Deepa's face like a book and would know if she was lying.

'He's nice, but there's nothing serious going on.'

'Hmmm.' Shanta didn't seem convinced. She refused to take her eyes off Deepa. She wanted the truth.

'Well, even if there was a chance of something happening, there's not a hope in hell of it now 'cos Bela's gone and ruined it all,' Deepa blurted out.

She went on to explain everything that had happened.

'But Bela doesn't seem like that type of girl,' commented Shanta, once Deepa had got to the end of her story. 'Although, everything is possible in this industry.'

As Shanta mulled over whether Bela really could be responsible for such an act, the taxi pulled up into the car park of Starlight radio station.

'This interview is gonna be a nightmare, Mum,'

predicted Deepa. 'They're supposed to be talking about my career, but they'll just want to know about all this rubbish. What do I do?'

'Leave it to me,' said Shanta firmly. She grabbed hold of Deepa's hand and they made their way to the reception desk where there was an assistant waiting to greet them.

'This is Deepa Khanna and I am her mother. We are here for Deepa's interview, but before we start recording I need to speak to the producer of the show. It's urgent.' Shanta could be very commanding when she wanted to be.

The assistant nodded and then picked up the telephone on the reception desk. She called the producer and passed on the message.

'Producer *sahib* has requested that you to go to his office,' she informed Shanta and Deepa. 'I'll take you there.'

Shanta nodded. She linked arms with her daughter and they followed the girl.

'Let me do the talking,' Shanta whispered to Deepa.

'No problems there, Mum. I'm more than happy for you to do it,' smiled Deepa, relieved that her mum was taking control of the situation.

Shanta, usually a laidback and non-meddling

woman, had evidently decided she would have to be a bit more assertive here than she was in her own home. She tapped on the producer's door and then, without even waiting for a reply, turned the handle and marched in. After exchanging pleasantries with the man behind the desk Shanta announced: 'Deepa will not be answering any personal questions today. Please agree to that or she won't be doing the interview.'

Deepa looked up at her mum, shocked but pleasantly surprised at her no-nonsense stance.

'We're interested in Deepa's career, Mrs Khanna – nothing else. Trust me,' the producer assured Shanta.

'Good. So take us to the studio then, please. We don't have a great deal of time.'

'Now that that's sorted,' Shanta whispered to Deepa as they made their way to the recording studio, 'you'd better resolve matters with Ajay. If he's a nice guy, don't let misunderstandings get in the way of your friendship. Talk to him.'

Deepa looked at her mum and, for the first time in a while, felt her mood lift a little. She smiled. Deepa was starting to discover there was a lot more to her mum than she had ever realised, and she was delighted.

Chapter 5

Deepa stood and watched as Ajay performed a funky dance number with a bevy of beauties. He appeared to be moving effortlessly, but Deepa could see how much energy he was putting into every move. He was a real joy to watch.

She was waiting for Ajay's shot to end so she could have a word with him. If it hadn't been for her mum Deepa would never have come to Ajay's film set, but Shanta had convinced her that she needed to clear the air. Even if Ajay didn't want to date her any more, she had to let him know she wasn't a liar or a cheat.

The scene Ajay was shooting took place in a nightclub, so the lights around the studio were dimmed down and hardly anyone seemed to have noticed that Deepa was there.

Including Ajay.

As soon as a break was called, he began making his way back to his dressing room. Deepa followed him.

'Uhh, Ajay,' she murmured from behind.

He turned around.

'I need to talk to you,' she began nervously.

If he was surprised to see her, he didn't show it. 'Hi, Deepa. Talk to me? Sure. What about?' came his short reply.

'Just… things.'

'Without meaning to sound rude,' he said simply, 'I don't think there's much left to say.'

'Please, Ajay, hear me out at least.'

He stopped to ponder her request, but then his eye was drawn to a small group of people huddled together a few feet away. They were film extras and Deepa realised they were watching the couple and trying to work out what was being said.

'Right, okay… we can talk,' he agreed in a very business-like manner, 'but this isn't the place. I'm working right now and there are a lot of nosy people about. I'll meet you for a quick drink tonight. Do you know the Moonlight Café?'

Deepa nodded.

'I'll see you there. At seven.'

'Great, thanks. See you then.'

Ajay turned around and walked off, wiping the sweat from his neck with a towel that was hanging on a peg nearby. Deepa turned around and glanced at the film extras. They quickly turned their faces away when they saw her looking at them and she chuckled to herself.

Deepa was in a great mood now. It was a boiling hot day but she didn't mind. She hummed all the way back to her taxi and decided that when she got home she would spend the free time before her meeting with Ajay catching up with her old friends on a networking website and then calling her beautician over to give her a facial, a massage and some top-to-toe beauty treatment.

She also decided to stay upstairs in her bedroom, away from her dad. He would still be very angry with her for her public attack on Bela.

By six thirty, she was ready to go and meet Ajay and, after giving her mum a kiss, she tiptoed down the stairs and quietly left the house. She wasn't quite as excited as she had been a few nights ago – this café meeting wasn't exactly a midnight moonlight tryst. Still, it was better than nothing and Deepa felt she had to give it a go.

Dressed in a burgundy skirt with floaty cream blouse, Deepa arrived at the Moonlight Café at six fifty and decided to wait outside, at one of the round, silver tables. She sat down, pushed her sunglasses on to her head and ordered a Coca-cola. She then pulled a romantic novel out of her bag. Deepa didn't get beyond chapter one, though; it wasn't long before Ajay arrived. He was wearing a baseball cap and designer shades, and was talking to somebody on the phone as he neared her.

'Yes, I'll do the show,' he said, raising his index finger to indicate to Deepa he'd only be a minute.

She smiled in acknowledgement.

'Holland and UK are fine. Two dates each. Which other stars have confirmed?'

Deepa kept her eyes on the pages of her book but she wasn't reading now; she was much more interested to know what this show was, and whether she would be invited to perform too.

'Okay, so Monica and Shantipriya are booked. And Marc. *Mmm hmm.* Right then, it's a done deal. Send the contracts to my agent and I'll speak to you in a few weeks about rehearsals.' He then flipped his phone shut.

'Sorry,' apologised Ajay. 'Had to take the call.'

'It's okay,' she smiled. 'I was going to say take your time – work comes first. Are you doing an overseas tour?'

Ajay nodded. He then turned around and waved at a waiter, trying to catch his attention.

'What would you like, sir?'

Ajay looked at Deepa. 'Coke again, please.'

'Same for me,' said Ajay. 'But we need a table inside. A private one.'

The waiter nodded, then led them to the far end of the restaurant where they were unlikely to be disturbed. Deepa's heart was beating fast as she thought about how to broach the topic she was here to discuss.

She needn't have worried. Ajay got straight to the point.

'So, what are we here for, Deepa? What do you want to say?'

Deepa peered up at him. Her dark eyes focused on his gorgeous face, searching for some affection. Last time they'd met by the steps of the Clock Tower, he'd been very cold towards her. She was desperate to see if his feelings had softened at all.

'I wouldn't have had the nerve to come here if I'd lied to you about that night,' Deepa began, earnestly.

There were a few youngsters piling into the restaurant now and Deepa shifted her chair slightly so her face couldn't be seen. She realised they needed to get the conversation over and done with fairly quickly before they were spotted.

'If I'd lied or cheated on you, I would have just stayed away. I wouldn't be pleading with you, trying to explain myself,' she reasoned. 'Think about it, Ajay; does the girl that Bela described even sound like me?'

Ajay stared at Deepa. He didn't say a word but he seemed to be prepared to listen at least.

'I don't know why Bela said what she did and I don't know what she saw, but I wasn't out that night,' continued Deepa. 'I haven't been messing around with anyone else. Even though you and I weren't exactly in a relationship, it was heading that way. If

I'd wanted to see other guys I would have told you. I didn't need to pretend I was home when I was out.'

Ajay looked down and fiddled around with a set of keys he'd just taken out of his pocket.

'I'm telling you this because I don't want to have this misunderstanding between us, Ajay,' Deepa implored, sensing she wasn't getting through to him as she'd hoped. 'Okay, so you don't want to hang out with me any more – fair enough. But we'll soon be working on a film together, and there might be more. We need to clear the air.'

Ajay was still silent. Deepa looked eagerly at him, waiting for a response. She had her hands folded in front of her on the table. It was like waiting for an exam result.

'Hmmm.' He leaned back in his chair and looked Deepa in the eye. 'Okay. What can I say? I guess I'll have to take your word for it.'

Deepa's eye widened. The tension drained away from her body but she didn't dare get too hopeful yet. She wasn't sure if Ajay really was going to give her the benefit of the doubt. He might just be saying that to get her off his back.

She needn't have worried. 'I'm sorry I reacted so badly,' he started. 'But I couldn't understand why you didn't take my calls. And then I heard you were out with this other guy and it all seemed to make sense.' Ajay shook his head as he thought through what had happened. 'Bela swore it was you… And then someone else I know mentioned it too, so I had no reason not to believe it.'

'It's so weird,' said Deepa, mystified. 'I must admit I've been hearing a lot of this kind of stuff over the past few days too. Maybe there really is someone out there who looks just like me… it's possible, I suppose,' she acknowledged. 'Maybe Bela was genuinely mistaken. And then I went and had a go at her… Oh dear.'

'You see, Deepa?' said Ajay, his tone now softer. 'I had a go at you without checking the facts and you've done the same thing to Bela. We're both guilty of making the same mistake. What do you say? Can we wipe the slate clean and start afresh?'

Deepa nodded and smiled. She still felt bad about her altercation with Bela but she could sort that out later. Right now, there was more important business to attend to.

Ajay offered his hand in friendship and Deepa shook it, beaming widely. He then clasped both of his hands tightly around hers and pulled her towards him. They gazed lovingly into each other's eyes and Ajay moved his face closer until the tip of his nose touched hers. Deepa giggled and cocked her head shyly to one side. She looked up again and edged closer still, but then something caught her eye that made her blood run cold.

She froze.

'Don't worry about the customers, they haven't seen us yet,' said Ajay. 'Relax.'

But Ajay's words were wasted on Deepa – she wasn't looking at the customers, or even listening to him. She was gazing straight through the café's huge window to where a figure stood staring at her. It was the same mysterious old man she'd spotted twice before.

Deepa now knew it was no coincidence.

She was definitely being followed.

* * *

'Don't worry, Deepa. Are you sure you couldn't be mistaken?' said Ajay as he comforted her in his car a few moments later.

'No, definitely not,' said Deepa firmly. 'I know it was him. I've seen his face before… He was looking at me through the window when we were doing that modelling shoot. And then I saw him again in the empty TV studio a few days ago. And now he's here… it's… it's awful… it's creepy.' She shuddered.

Ajay gently put his arm around Deepa. She looked really scared and he was concerned. After running his fingers through his hair, mussing up the style that was his trademark, he put his head next to hers. 'Try not to worry. Just think of it like this: you're nobody in this business until you've got a crazy fan. This just means you've hit the big time.'

Deepa took a sharp intake of breath. 'I know what you mean, Ajay, but believe me, this is not like having a keen fan. I've been getting loads of letters every day since *Mumbai Magic,* some from teenage boys, some from older men, some from girls. I've even had three or four marriage proposals. But none of those people have ever followed me around like this. It's not the same thing.'

Ajay acknowledged what she was saying with a nod.

'And what about the way he ran off as soon as I pointed him out to you?' continued Deepa. 'It's too bad you were facing the other direction in the café. If you'd seen him, you'd know it was the same man who was peeping when we shot the *FilmGlitz* cover.'

'Look, Deepa,' Ajay interjected. 'There are these three girls who come and stand outside my house every day after school – they can't be older than fifteen. They come at four o'clock sharp. It's weird, but you're in a business where things like this happen. In fact it would be weirder if they didn't.'

Deepa nodded, trying her best to be rational.

'On the other hand,' Ajay added, his tone of voice more serious now. 'Chances are, these girls are harmless. They hang around for a while and then go. As for your guy, we don't know. You're a young woman and you need to be much more cautious until you're certain he's not a threat. Don't travel alone until you know for sure that he's not a psycho.'

Deepa's stomach lurched. She took a gulp and sat staring through the windscreen.

'Let's take you home, Deeps,' decided Ajay, realising he might just have made things worse. He started the engine.

'Stalker.'

'Hmmm?' asked Ajay, as he drove off.

'I've got a stalker… Oh my God!' exclaimed Deepa, raising a hand to her mouth. 'What if he starts turning up everywhere I go? I won't be able to do anything! He must know where I live… And I've been going around on my own – here, there and everywhere. He's probably following me all the time. Oh my God! I feel sick!' she cried, holding her head in her hands.

'Calm down, Deepa,' said Ajay, stopping the car

and putting his hand on her knee. 'There's no point in getting all hysterical about it. We'll deal with it,' he added, looking into her eyes and trying to reassure her. 'Just make sure you're accompanied from now on. As long as you don't go out and about on your own, you'll be fine.'

Deepa nodded but she wasn't at all happy. 'Let's go,' she murmured.

She was keen to get back home, but at the same time she was worried about telling her parents and about how they would react to the awful news.

* * *

'What?' spat Deepa's dad, across the dining table later that evening. 'What the hell are you talking about? A stalker? You?'

Deepa looked at him, shocked and disappointed by his reaction. 'I should have known you'd react like this,' she said. 'Why couldn't you be concerned, instead of just belittling me yet again? Why wouldn't someone be following me? It's not that ridiculous and far-fetched, is it?'

'Yes, Jayant. You must take this seriously,' insisted Shanta, untying her apron and taking a seat next to her daughter. 'It's very worrying. Try to understand,' she said to her husband.

'But she's not even a proper star yet!' Jayant roared. 'She's only had one hit – which reminds me, the producer of *Betaabi* said he wants you to go to the Shamsher Hotel for a big pre-release launch party at the end of next month. That's going to be the big test. If this film doesn't click, we'll be back to square one – worrying about money all over again.'

Deepa shook her head in disbelief. 'Dad, all you care about is money, money and money!' she screamed, standing up and slamming her hand on the table.

This was most unlike Deepa and even her dad was shocked.

'Ever since I was little, all I've heard about is how your "investment in me" has to pay off and how I have to make you all financially secure,' she continued. 'You're so mean to me! I don't know anybody else who has had to put up with this much pressure and be forced into a career that would never have been their first choice!'

Deepa was raging. She had never stood up to her father like this before, and now all her pent-up emotions came flooding out.

Jayant sat and listened, gathering his thoughts. Now, it was his turn.

'The problem with you is that you're spoilt and

utterly ungrateful,' he summarised. His arms were folded tightly across his chest. 'We've had to make many sacrifices to get you to where you are, do you understand? A career you never wanted to follow – *phuh*!'

'Shhh, keep your voice down, *ji*. The neighbours will hear you,' Shanta pleaded, while Sachin decided he wasn't hungry after all and quietly left the table.

'Shanta, be quiet!' ordered Jayant, standing up and turning towards his wife to vent his anger on her. 'I don't care about the damned neighbours – let them hear exactly how spoilt this so-called star is!' He turned back to Deepa, 'All parents send their kids to school knowing it's good for their future. Most kids don't want to go, but are their parents wrong to send them?'

Deepa made no response.

Jayant took off his glasses and slammed them on the table. 'Answer me!'

The high pitch of his voice made Deepa flinch and she quickly sat down. 'No,' she admitted in a tiny voice.

'So what if someone's following you?' said Jayant. 'We'll investigate it, we'll go with you wherever you go and we'll protect you. But don't *ever* say I forced you into this career – this is every girl's dream!'

He took a few steps closer to her. 'What did you want to do anyway?' he probed. 'Become a nursery assistant like that Shobha friend of yours? Or a shopkeeper like Puja? Ninety nine per cent of girls would give their right arm to be where you are today. Walk away now and I will *never* speak to you again! Understand?'

Jayant stood over Deepa's chair staring at her. By now, Deepa was trying not to cry. The first wave of her emotions had come out as anger, but now her feelings were welling up again in the middle of her chest and she knew she couldn't contain the tears for much longer.

'Try and understand,' said Shanta again, this time tugging gently at her husband's shirt. 'It could be anyone. *Anyone.*'

Jayant turned to his wife who raised her eyebrows in a significant look. They held each other's gaze for a moment, neither of them saying a word, and then Jayant slumped heavily into his chair and covered his eyes with his hand.

Deepa looked at her father and then her mother, but neither of them seemed to even remember that she was there. She retreated silently from the dining room, went up to her bedroom and fell on her bed where she sobbed her heart out.

Chapter 6

'Oh my goodness, so many cases!' exclaimed Shanta as she eyed the baggage belonging to the cast and crew of *Superstar*.

The twenty-strong team was travelling to Goa

from Mumbai's busy domestic airport and Deepa had decided to take her mum with her on the shoot. Her parents would never have let her travel so far afield on her own anyway, but now, with the stalker lurking, Deepa was actually pleased to have her mother as chaperone. Ajay, who was filming another project in South India, was due to meet up with the team in Goa the following day.

Vikram Sinha, the movie's production manager, gathered everyone together and once he had ticked everybody off his list, he led them to the Fly India check-in desks.

'Luckily, we haven't got any huge stars like Ajay with us today or we'd be surrounded by fans,' said Vikram to Jannat, his pretty, young assistant.

Unluckily for Vikram, Shanta overheard.

'Sorry, Vikram *sahib*,' Shanta snapped at him from behind, 'but isn't my daughter a huge star now? She's certainly being paid the top rate!'

Vikram turned around quickly. 'Aunti*ji*, I didn't mean to offend you. When I said "big star", I meant "superstar"–someone like Ajay Banerjee, Shantipriya or Bela, for instance.

'Hmm, so Bela's a superstar, is she?' Shanta pulled a face. 'Well, Deepa is not far behind. And anyway, the only reason we aren't getting swamped here is because of the effort she's made to disguise herself.'

Vikram cut a glance in Deepa's direction, looking her up and down. 'Oh, you mean the floppy straw hat and shades? Sorry, I didn't realise it was a disguise – looks more like fancy dress to me,' he commented sarcastically. He then shrugged his shoulders and carried on walking.

'More than I can say for your costume!' Shanta shot back.

Deepa looked at her mother and giggled. 'I don't understand you, Mum. You're such a mouse at home but such a big cat outside. Really!'

'When I was young I was always this outspoken,' Shanta declared proudly. 'But living with your father has taught me there are other ways of getting what you want too.'

'Get a move on, girls. You'll miss the plane at this rate!' reprimanded Vikram. Deepa and Shanta stepped up their pace and rushed to board the jet.

Following a short but luxurious flight, the film crew landed at Goa's bustling international airport.

Deepa waited with the rest of the team for the luggage to arrive in the baggage hall. She looked around at all the people milling around, some very excited at the prospect of discovering what this world-famous tourist resort had to offer.

'Is that Deepa Khanna – one of the actresses from *Mumbai Magic*?'

Deepa looked around to see who had recognised her. It was a young girl waiting by the baggage conveyor belt with her parents.

'Will she sign my book?' the girl asked her mum.

'Would you like an autograph?' Deepa said, walking over to the girl.

The young fan nodded keenly and Deepa took a pen from her bag. 'There you go,' she said, as she handed the signed book back to her. The girl's face lit up and she showed it off to her dad who thanked Deepa.

'Right, Miss Deepa Khanna, please stop drawing attention to yourself or you'll have a whole crowd of autograph hunters in no time and then we'll have a security problem on our hands,' moaned Vikram once he realised what was going on.

Shanta gave Vikram a moody stare, but Deepa felt a bit embarrassed and hurriedly put her hat and shades back on.

'Okay, everybody. Make your way to that big yellow sign just outside the building over there,' said Vikram, pointing. 'There's our coach.'

The crew members shuffled around and walked towards the sign. Then, one by one, they all piled into the big coach that was waiting to take them to their hotel.

Once seated inside, Deepa looked out of the window, eager to see what Goa was like. She immediately sensed that the pace of life was much slower here than in Mumbai. There was less traffic, the buildings were smaller – as well as fewer and further between – and the people seemed to amble around rather than rushing as they went about their daily business.

It all felt very lazy and peaceful, and the troubles back home in Mumbai – her dad, the stalker and all the mysterious sightings of the girl who looked like her – seemed as distant as the big city itself.

When the coach pulled up outside the Indian Heritage Hotel, a five-star holiday resort, everyone was impressed, and some people even gasped. It looked extremely luxurious. The marble building had a huge entrance that featured two gold-plated statues of lions and the extensive gardens were immaculately manicured. The whole complex was surrounded by a moat.

'Gosh, it's amazing, isn't it? Although it doesn't exactly fit in with the surroundings.' said Deepa as she marvelled at it. 'It could be a hotel anywhere in the world.'

'Yeah, you're right,' agreed Shanta. 'I certainly don't feel like I'm in India right now. I'm curious to see what the inside's like.'

'And you will see it very soon if you all stop talking,' said Vikram rudely, as he moved to the front of the coach. 'Before you lot all start trying to jump off, can the production unit and their guests please wait in the lobby area? You will all be staying in the Bridge Wing,' he informed them, reading from an A4 notepad. 'The cast of the film and their guests will be staying in the Lakeside Wing. You can make your own way down now. It's signposted and should be easy to get to. Luggage will be sent to your rooms.'

Deepa and Shanta set off towards the Lakeside Wing along with the other cast members and their families. As they passed one of the superb Olympic-sized pools in the complex, a young man, an employee at the hotel, looked up and started walking in the same direction as Deepa.

Deepa kept her eye on him as she walked, and started to feel there was something a bit odd about this boy. He seemed to be following her in particular. He was certainly making an effort to keep pace with her. Each time she walked faster or slowed down a bit, he did too. So she stopped in her tracks, just to see what would happen then. Bad move. Sahil Walia, the actor who was playing her father in Superstar, walked straight into her.

'*Ooof!*' he burst out as Deepa lunged forward, dropping her small make-up case on the ground.

'Sorry, Sahil *sahib*,' apologised Deepa.

'No problem,' he replied politely. 'I guess I need to keep my distance.'

She stopped to pick up her case, but was beaten to it by the hotel employee. 'Hey *banjaaran*,' he whispered to her. 'Will you dance for me today?'

Deepa looked at him in shock. 'Excuse me?' she cried, quickly getting up. 'Mum, did you hear that? He called me *banjaaran*, he thinks I'm a gypsy! He asked me to dance for him!'

'Huh? Did he?' asked Shanta.

'Yes!'

Shanta turned to look at the man. 'Apologise, then get out of here before we get you sacked, you dirty, good-for-nothing scoundrel!' she yelled, removing one of her sandals in readiness to beat him. 'Don't you know who Deepa Khanna is? She's not a gypsy – she's a movie star!'

The man ran off and all the people in the group huddled round Deepa, noisily discussing what had happened.

'It's okay… it was nothing,' said Deepa to one of her co-stars, keen to avoid a big scene. 'He called me a gypsy and I was a bit taken aback. But he didn't do anything.'

'Who is he?' asked someone else.

'He's gone now,' said Deepa. 'Please don't make a big deal of it. Let's just go.'

But it was too late; somebody had already called the hotel manager. A woman in a smart suit arrived and Shanta turned her anger on her. A couple of the other mothers joined in too.

'Is this how you train your staff to behave?' Shanta demanded. 'My daughter is a famous actress. And we're not gypsies! I want you to discipline that young man. How dare he approach my daughter and then insult her? It's outrageous!'

'Mum, please just forget it.'

'No! He was very rude. I'm not going to ignore that. How can you forget someone calling you a gypsy?'

'I am very sorry for your distress, Madam, and I assure you that we will look into the matter and deal with it,' apologised the hotel manager. She was very embarrassed and keen to calm the situation down as soon as possible – a small crowd of hotel guests had gathered to watch the unfolding drama. 'Please let me show you to your rooms, you must be very tired,' the hotel manager continued. 'And then I will personally look into this matter myself. Your complaint will be treated with the utmost seriousness.'

Shanta pulled the loose end of her saree tightly around her and nodded. Deepa heaved a sigh of relief and quickly linked arms with her mum to make sure she carried on walking.

Once they reached their room, Deepa slumped face down on to her huge triple-sized bed. 'Gosh, that was embarrassing,' she mumbled into a pillow. 'Some people are so rude, but Mum,' she added, looking up, 'you really mustn't create a scene like that every time someone says something you don't like. I know I said I was impressed by your assertive side, but don't overdo it.'

'No, we have to stand up to these slimeballs,' said Shanta. 'This is a five-star hotel – you think the hotel manager doesn't need to know what the staff is like?'

'Yeah, I get it,' said Deepa wearily. 'But perhaps it would be easier just to ignore these stray comments. People are always gonna say things... although I do think it's strange that he called me a gypsy. Why would he say that?'

Shanta didn't have a chance to reply because at that moment, Deepa's mobile phone rang out. It was Ajay. Excited, she ran out to the balcony to answer it.

'Hi Ajay, we just arrived,' she said, looking out to the sea. 'Are you still in Kerala?'

'Sure am, but I'll be with you tomorrow. Just wanted to check you're fine – nothing strange going on, I hope.'

'Well, apart from someone calling me a gypsy as soon as I arrived…!' she laughed. 'But no stalker as far as I can see – thank goodness.'

'Someone called you a gypsy?' Ajay asked. 'That's odd. Why would they do that?'

'I don't know. It was just a worker from the hotel… Chat-up lines are different in Goa, I guess,' she joked. Talking to Ajay about it made her see the funny side.

'Is your mum with you?' asked Ajay.

Deepa peered back into the room. Shanta was lying on the bed, facing away from the window and was obviously exhausted by the day's travel. Although Deepa couldn't see her face, she suspected her mother had fallen asleep.

'Yeah, Mum's with me. She wouldn't have let me come on my own – especially at the moment,' whispered Deepa. 'It's good she's here though, she's cool. I'm sure you and I will be able to go out and about without too much trouble.'

'Of course, you mustn't travel alone now,' said Ajay. 'I would've been mad if you hadn't brought her along. But I'd better go, I'm only on a five-minute break. See you tomorrow, babe.'

'Okay, see you tomorrow then. Bye.'

Deepa had acted cool and collected while on the phone to Ajay, but hearing him call her 'babe' made her heart skip a beat. They'd been through a rough patch, but Deepa felt it might even have brought them closer. Singing happily away to herself, the teenage heroine skipped back inside the room, showered, changed and hit the sack.

* * *

The next morning, Deepa woke up bright and early. As soon as she opened her eyes she remembered that Ajay was arriving, and after that there was no chance of her falling asleep again.

Shanta had already got dressed and ordered room service so it wasn't long before mother and daughter were enjoying a continental breakfast on the sun terrace. Deepa smiled as she feasted her eyes on a beautiful stretch of Goan beach set against a backdrop of palm trees. She felt very relaxed and was ready to enjoy every moment of this trip.

'Why can't every morning be like this, Mum? Wouldn't it be bliss?'

'Sure would, *beti*,' she replied, sipping tea. 'Enjoy it while you can. It's just a shame we couldn't bring Sachin along too. He'd love all this.'

'Yeah, but his studies are really important now.'

'I know,' agreed Shanta. 'But how about asking your dad to come next time?'

Deepa gave her mum a wide-eyed, horror-filled look.

'Your poor dad!' exclaimed Shanta. 'He's not that bad! I'm serious, we should think about inviting him. It might make him relax a bit… he may even change his ways.'

'Miracles can happen, I suppose,' laughed Deepa, biting into a croissant. Aware that she didn't have a lot of time to play with, she finished eating quickly and then slipped into a pair of pedal pushers and a plain, fitted T-shirt. After applying some light make-up to her flawless skin, she and Shanta ventured into the lobby area where Vikram was waiting to give the crew a briefing.

Vikram was sitting in the middle of a huge pink sofa, surrounded by the character actors who were playing minor roles in the film. 'Aah, Deepa,' he said when he spotted her. 'We're waiting for your stylist to show. Tomorrow morning we'll be shooting a song sequence on a beach in the South. You'll need to wear a selection of swimsuits and do your best to look real hot, okay?'

'Nothing too revealing I hope, Vikram *sahib*,' Deepa said, plonking her bag down on the floor while she looked around for two seats.

'Nothing that a top heroine wouldn't wear,' he bolted back.

'So you mean to say that if the top actresses reveal their bosoms and bottoms, Deepa will automatically do the same?' Shanta piped up.

'Mum,' said Deepa. 'Please, leave this to me.'

'Yes Mummy*ji*, please heed your daughter's advice before you and I get off on the wrong foot. We've got a lot to get through while we're here and we're already running late. So, if you don't mind, I'd appreciate it if you'd take a step back.'

As it happened, though, Shanta did mind, and definitely didn't take kindly to being called Mummy*ji* by a man hardly younger than herself. She realised she was losing patience with Vikram but didn't want to cause Deepa any more trouble, so she found one of the other star mums to talk to and both women went and sat in the far corner of the reception area.

'Sorry, Vikram *sahib*,' puffed a voice at the hotel entrance.

It was Amrita, out of breath and with a huge pile of clothes slung over each arm.

'Just landed this morning, my flight was a bit late… But here are Deepa's outfits, and I have some photos of what I want her hair to look like.'

'Oh well, better late than never,' Vikram muttered as he grabbed the bits of paper from Amrita and passed them to his assistant, Jannat. 'Hang on to these,' he ordered, before standing up to address the people seated in front of him.

'Right, I've printed out some schedule sheets – please read them carefully. We only have a week to complete the shoot so we can't afford any delays. Deepa, go and try the clothes on, please. You need three outfits for the song. Take Amrita with you. Then Ajay's stylist will need to select his shirt and trousers according to the colours you choose.'

'Yes, sir,' said Amrita obediently. Vikram cut her a stern glance, suspicious that she might be teasing him.

Deepa led Amrita to her room to finalise their selection of clothes while Shanta and her new friend settled down with masala tea and samosas, having already found plenty to gossip about.

'You should have seen the look on his face!' exclaimed Deepa, filling Amrita in on the bitter exchange of words that had just taken place between her mum and Vikram.

'I heard he's a complete control freak!' laughed Amrita. 'So it's probably good that your mum put him in his place. I was tempted to say something myself, but you would just end up taking the rap for it so I decided against it.'

'We've got days of this to go – I can really see things escalating. God help us!' said Deepa, as she put her key card into the door to open it.

She entered the room and took a sharp intake of breath.

The patio door at the far end was wide open and the full-length net curtain was being blown about by the wind.

Deepa grabbed Amrita's hand as she walked further into the room and her eyes lit upon an empty carrier bag that sat on the middle of the bed. It didn't belong to her or her mum, she was sure.

'Oh no,' she whispered.

'What's up?' asked Amrita, looking around. 'Something wrong?'

'Someone's been in here,' said Deepa, and she felt the blood drain away from her face. She wanted to run out of the room, but her feet didn't move.

'Are you sure? How do you know?'

Deepa squeezed Amrita's hand even tighter. 'We didn't leave the door open, I double-checked that it was locked... and that carrier bag's not mine,' she explained. 'And look at the stuff on the dressing table... it's been knocked down. I arranged it all neatly.'

'That could just be the wind.'

'But what about the door?' Deepa asked.

'Maybe your mum opened it after you locked it,' reasoned Amrita, trying to be rational, but also feeling a little afraid. 'Or maybe it was the cleaner.'

Desperate for a logical explanation, Deepa ran into the bathroom. She shook her head as she realised it hadn't been cleaned – the towel she had left on the floor after her shower was still there. And then she caught sight of the muddy footprints.

'Oh my God,' mumbled Deepa as a cold shiver ran up her spine. 'It must be him... it's him... he's here!' She ran out of the bedroom, leaving Amrita behind.

'Mum!' she screamed as she fled to the reception area, with Amrita chasing close behind.

Deepa bolted through the double doors, past Vikram and the crew and grabbed her mum's arm, spilling tea over her saree.

Amrita ran in a few moments later and tried to explain Deepa's hysteria to Vikram who wasn't at all pleased at having his meeting interrupted.

'What's all this nonsense, Deepa?' Vikram started as he walked over to her. 'How can someone follow you all the way from Mumbai to Goa and end up in this hotel within a day of you arriving? There's been no publicity whatsoever. No-one knows you're here. You must have left the door open yourself,' he decided. 'Or it could have been the cleaner who hasn't got round to the bathroom yet or even a stray animal. Please be rational.'

Deepa, who was crouching down on the floor by her mum's chair, lifted her head and looked at Vikram through her tear-filled eyes. 'It's him… I just know it,' she sobbed.

'Take her seriously will you!' Shanta shrieked at Vikram as a small crowd of onlookers gathered around. Most of the people were foreign tourists and didn't know who Deepa was, but they all wanted to find out what had upset this beautiful young girl.

'Auntiji, I AM taking her seriously. I'm just trying to think of what else could be at the centre of this.'

'I *know* who it is!' sobbed Deepa. 'Why won't you listen?'

And then suddenly, as if he'd heard her cry for help, there was Ajay walking through the hotel's revolving door, wearing a bright pink half-sleeved shirt and white trousers.

Without planning to, or even thinking of the consequences, Deepa ran towards him. 'Ajay! He's been here but nobody believes me! Tell them, tell them!' She grabbed him tightly.

'Okay... okay... calm down, Deepa,' said Ajay, pulling back from her grip and moving towards the film crew. It wasn't that he didn't want to hug her, but he was still in control of himself in a way that Deepa wasn't, and he realised this wasn't the right place or time.

'I was at a photo shoot and then somewhere else with Deepa last week. The same man turned up at both places, just to stare at her through windows, it seems,' Ajay said to Vikram. 'Deepa also saw him at a TV studio where she was being interviewed. She's really worried he might be a stalker and I think we need to take her concerns seriously.'

Vikram looked at Ajay, intrigued. He had recognised immediately that the friendship between Deepa and Ajay went a lot further than a simple working relationship.

'Okay, you guys sort this out,' Vikram said after a few moments. 'The rest of you can take some time out, but be ready to meet back here at two o'clock sharp. And be prepared for some serious work! We have to complete the promotional scenes today or the schedule has had it!'

The crew dispersed while Ajay, Deepa and Shanta walked over to the reception desk to make enquiries about whether a cleaner had been to the room or not. Apparently, nobody had been to clean the suite that morning.

'I told you!' exclaimed Deepa, looking back and forth between Ajay and her mum. 'I knew it!'

'Okay, Deepa,' said Ajay. 'We've got a problem here, we recognise that. Now we have to decide how best to deal with it.'

Deepa nodded. She was horrified at the confirmation that there had been an intruder in her hotel room, but she was glad that Ajay at least was taking her seriously. Vikram seemed to be convinced that she was just paranoid, and the rest of the crew probably thought the same.

'Okay, what do you suggest?' Deepa asked.

'Let's call the police,' said Ajay and Shanta simultaneously.

'It's important that they know about this,' Ajay went on. 'We have to keep an open mind, Deepa. This intruder could have been somebody other than the stalker – an opportunistic fan or a thief. But until we know for sure, you need security.'

Deepa's mind was racing and she sat down on the pink sofa to think while Ajay got the receptionist to call the police.

'What a mess!' cried Shanta. 'Thank God that Ajay is here, though. Nobody else even seems to care, especially that Vikram *shikram*.'

Deepa tried to force a smile to show she was glad her mum had taken a liking to Ajay, but she couldn't manage it. She just sat in silence until a senior police officer arrived.

He took a report of the incident and asked Deepa to give a description of the man's physical features. The room that Deepa had been staying in was then cordoned off and a team of officers searched it for clues.

Deepa and Shanta were moved to a different room and a police guard was stationed outside. Although Deepa felt uncomfortable about being treated differently from everybody else, she was seriously concerned for her own safety and was glad of the police protection.

Double Take

She managed to forget about her troubles for a few hours during the afternoon while they were filming the trailer for the movie, but when darkness fell it was a different story.

Even with the policeman standing outside her door Deepa felt vulnerable, and when she went to bed that night and closed her eyes, she could see nothing but an image of the man with his dark, troubled expression staring at her...

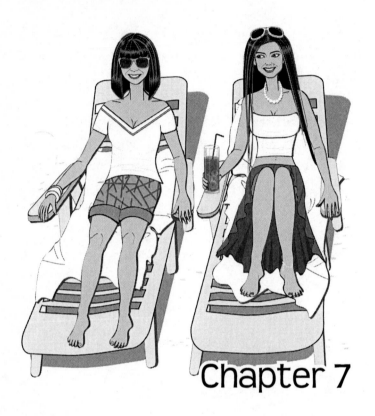

Chapter 7

The next morning, though, sitting on the beach and relaxing on a sun lounger with a long, cool drink in her hand, Deepa felt one hundred per cent different from how she had the night before.

'Yeah, I'm still worried,' she told Amrita as the two girls looked out to the beautiful blue ocean, 'but nothing can happen while there's a police guard with me all the time. He seems very nice as well

– his name's Aman. He's in that car over there, permanently staring at me.'

'Well, that's his job, isn't it?'

'I suppose so, but this whole thing is just so weird,' said Deepa.

'What do you mean?'

'Well, why has this stalker targeted me in the first place?'

'Hey, you're beautiful, remember!' Amrita reminded her. 'You haven't got Ajay running around after you for nothing!'

Deepa smiled. 'Thanks for the confidence boost, but there are all sorts of more popular, more beautiful girls than me in this industry. Do they have problems like this as well?'

'All stars do, honey,' said Amrita, leaning back and closing her eyes. 'Just enjoy being here and try not to think about it too much.'

'Oh, I am enjoying it, in spite of all this,' said Deepa. 'It's so much more relaxing than Mumbai, isn't it? Why can't the industry move here?'

'Ready to start, girls?' interrupted Vikram, as he approached them. As usual, he was armed with a huge clipboard. 'I need you to start getting ready for the first segment of the song with the… ummm… did we say green outfit, Amrita?'

'Yes,' she confirmed.

'Right, so it's the green outfit first. You have an hour to get ready, although you should only need half that time. Make sure you're back here by eleven o'clock. There's your trailer, Deepa,' he said, pointing over to his left.

Deepa looked up at what seemed to be more like a caravan than a movie star's trailer. She gathered up her belongings from the sunlounger and began making her way towards it with Amrita.

'I can't wait to start shooting this song,' said Deepa excitedly. 'It's meant to be one of the best in the whole movie. It's got a really good summer vibe.'

'Yeah, and Ajay's turned into a great dancer, hasn't he?' said Amrita. 'You'll have to work to keep up, madam.'

'Yes, I know. I am a bit nervous about that, actually, but I'll just have to really focus. I don't want Ajay thinking I'm hopeless,' said Deepa. 'Just the thought of being up there with him on the silver screen makes me determined to do well.'

When they reached the trailer, Amrita turned the door handle and stepped up to go inside. 'Oh!' she exclaimed. 'It's not at all bad in here, it's quite neat. Much better than it looks on the outside. Vikram had me worried for a bit.'

Deepa looked around and was also surprised to see that the mobile dressing room was light and airy, and smartly decked out with contemporary red furniture. She went to the dressing area to get changed. She took off her gypsy skirt and vest top but just as she was about to slip into her tight, green mini skirt with matching bra-top, she glimpsed Ajay through the window. He must have been walking to his own trailer and happened to look up, whereupon he spied Deepa. She quickly ducked.

'Oh my God!' Deepa shrieked. 'I think he saw me – naked!'

'Who?'

'Ajay!'

'So dramatic, Miss Deepa Khanna,' laughed Amrita as she unravelled the lead of her straightening tongs. 'But you're not naked – that's perfectly good underwear.'

Deepa stayed crouched down on the floor and reached her arm up to the red and white curtains that framed the window. She hastily tugged them closed.

'I'm gonna be so embarrassed now, knowing that Ajay has seen me in my undies! How awful is that?'

'Well, it might have been worse – just be glad it wasn't Vikram,' joked Amrita. 'Get over it, darling, and hurry up! We need to sort your hair out as soon as you're dressed.'

'Yes okay, here we go,' said Deepa squeezing herself into the outfit. She couldn't imagine a tighter fit. Her bust was almost spilling out of the top and the skirt was like a second skin.

Taking a deep breath, she sat down to let Amrita get to work. Deepa had such lustrous hair, the job was easy. Amrita simply straightened it, finished it with a shining agent and then took a section from the front and pinned it to the side of her head with a butterfly clip.

'How's that?' asked Amrita as she took a big mirror out of her vanity bag and held it up.

'Fab,' said Deepa, turning her head so she could see her face from all angles. 'Simple, but stylish. Let's go and show off!'

The girls giggled and chatted as they made their way back to the beach to find a convertible sports car parked on the sand and four dancers sporting bikinis striking various poses around it. Ajay sat in the driving seat, looking cool in a pair of red shades, and a photographer was eagerly taking some shots.

'What's the cameraman for?' Deepa asked Amrita.

'More promotional pictures, I guess. Like you

said, this is a big number and since it allows for a good outdoor shoot it'll probably be used to plug the movie.'

Deepa looked carefully at the girls and saw that they each had stomachs as flat as boards and legs without a hint of cellulite. 'Oh no, I'm gonna look awful next to them, Amrita,' she said, quite concerned. 'They're stunning.'

'Don't worry about it, crazy woman!' replied Amrita. 'You'll be fine. They may be a bit more toned than you, but there's nothing wrong with your figure. You look gorgeous. Don't get like some of the top heroines, the really famous ones, who demand that all the pretty background girls be replaced by less good-looking ones!'

'Do they? That's mad!'

'Oh yes,' said Amrita. 'I've seen it happen a few times. They're paranoid about being upstaged.'

'Hmmm,' pondered Deepa. 'I could never do anything like that, even if I made it really big. You know, the more time I spend in this industry, the more I wonder whether I'm really cut out for it.'

'You don't have to become like everyone else,' advised Amrita, 'but you should be aware of the kind of stuff that goes on around here. You get to see a lot of stuff when you work behind the scenes like I do. When these movie stars are stripped down, looking really bad without make-up and all that, it's amazing what they're prepared to tell you.'

Amrita shared some of her inside knowledge with Deepa, including the story of the actor who was having a relationship with a film producer's wife, while they waited for the cameras to be set up and the makeshift pier to be erected. Vikram came by a little while later and told Deepa to go and stand by the car. Amrita headed back to the sunlounger.

'The pier looks nice, doesn't it?' said Deepa to Ajay. The other dancers had moved away to be briefed by their agent so the couple were alone for a moment. 'Not sure it looks like it belongs in Goa, but it's nice all the same.'

'Not quite as nice as you,' he smiled, looking her up and down. 'You look damn hot!'

'Hey Ajay, not here please!' giggled Deepa.

'What do you mean not here? We're gonna be smooching and declaring our love for each other on that pier in a bit. I'm just getting myself in the mood.'

'Are we?' she asked. 'I wish they'd give us more detail about what we're supposed to be doing in these scenes. I feel a bit lost. It's always so last-minute, isn't it?'

'Hey, this is Bollywood, baby! What do you expect? You hoping for weather reports and all that jazz? We just go with the flow and make it up as we go along.'

'Ajay! Deepa! Over here please!' It was Vikram, calling from the sidelines. Deepa noticed another man standing nearby, briefing the technicians. This must be Vijay Kaul, the director of the movie. He was very well known, but Deepa had never worked with him before and had no idea what he was like as a director or as a person.

'Vijay, can I have your attention for a moment, please?' asked Vikram.

The director turned around. 'Yes. What is it?'

'I just want to present our stars. Ajay, obviously needs no introduction…' Vikram said.

'That's right. It's nice to see you again, Ajay,' said Vijay, shaking his hand.

'But I don't think you've ever met Deepa, have you?' Vikram went on. 'So, Deepa, this is Vijay Kaul. Vijay, meet Deepa Khanna.'

'Aah, the lovely Deepa,' said Vijay, extending his hand as he moved towards her. Deepa suddenly felt very self-conscious in her revealing outfit, and shook his hand politely before looking away.

Vikram led Ajay away for some more promotional

shots with the fit dancers, leaving Deepa and Vijay standing alone.

'I've heard a lot about you,' Vijay commented. 'I liked your work in *Mumbai Magic.*'

'Really?' asked Deepa, trying to fold her arms in such a way that her midriff was covered up. 'Thank you.'

'I think we'll have fun working together, but I may just need to go through a few of the finer points with you.'

'Oh?' Deepa felt even more insecure. Vijay must have heard about her disastrous dance duet with Bela and probably felt she needed extra practice.

'Right now, we'll just go ahead, but we're only going to film a few segments of the song today. For some of the more complex scenes, I need a bit more from you but I can explain it all later. What time can we meet tonight?' he asked.

'Umm, let me check with my mum,' said Deepa, looking around to see where Shanta had got to. 'Aah, there she is,' said Deepa. She pointed at Shanta who was standing at the far end of the beach buying goods from street vendors who were probably no more than ten years old. 'I'll just check what time–'

'We don't need your mum to be there, Deepa,' said Vijay bluntly. 'You're old enough to make appointments on your own now, aren't you?'

Deepa blushed. She suddenly felt really stupid and didn't know what to say. 'Yes, Vijay *sahib*,' she began. 'I… I was just saying she should come with me because I had this small problem with a… sta–'

Deepa paused. She hated the word "stalker". 'Someone has been following me and my mum is a bit worried. She wants to accompany me everywhere I go.'

'Yes, I heard,' Vijay told her, lighting up a cigarette and flicking his match to the ground. It landed a few feet away and seemed to scar the otherwise unblemished yellow sand. 'But you have a guard, so use him. Come to my suite at nine o'clock, the guard can wait outside and we can talk.'

Deepa wanted to say 'no' but she couldn't make the word come out of her mouth. Instead, she just nodded, still looking at the burnt-out match on the sand. The tête-à-tête was over as Deepa was called for a quick run-through, and she had to put the whole conversation to the back of her mind.

Deepa stood attentively as she waited for the choreographer, Poppy, to show her what to do.

'Okay, so this is a fast, peppy number,' explained Poppy, 'but it's quite easy, so, Deepa, you can just concentrate on looking good. You need to come across as a bit stuck up, so try to be aloof but sexy at the same time – plenty of pouting. There are a few complex dance steps in the chorus, but they're mainly for Ajay.'

'Oh,' said Deepa, surprised but quite relieved that she didn't have to worry about whether she would match up to Ajay.

Poppy then showed Deepa what she wanted her to do.

Ajay was supposed to be expressing his feelings for Deepa in the song and had to hold her close to his chest and brush his lips past hers while she played hard to get.

It was much easier than Deepa had feared as there was so little actual dancing involved, and after a fun and successful thirty-minute rehearsal, they were all told to sit down while the make-up artists made their final rounds.

Deepa took a seat and Amrita got her make-up kit out. 'What was Vijay saying to you?' Amrita asked curiously.

'That he needs to talk to me about a few things. I thought he was going to say I need dance practice or something, but apparently it's to do with the more meaningful scenes.'

'Oh?' said Amrita, raising her eyebrows. She

added black liner to Deepa's eyes to create a really dramatic look.

'He said I need to meet him tonight at nine o'clock in his room. I'm a bit gutted because I thought I'd be able to go out for a drink or a meal with Ajay tonight. Mum's really taken to him so she wouldn't have minded.'

'Vijay wants you to go to his room? At nine?'

'Yeah. Why, is that odd?' asked Deepa.

'You know what that means, don't you?'

Deepa thought for a moment and then gasped. 'No! It's nothing like that! Don't be so…' She trailed off. She had been going to say daft, but maybe Amrita was right. Vijay had been adamant that Deepa come alone.

'Oh my God, Amrita!' Deepa panicked. 'What if he tries it on? What am I going to do?'

'Just keep away, if you can,' said Amrita ominously, as she powdered Deepa's face.

Deepa was horrified at the mere thought that Vijay might have designs on her. She contemplated telling Ajay about it, but she couldn't be sure and didn't want to make a fool of herself if she was wrong.

'I don't understand why so many people from around the world are so desperate to make it in

Bollywood,' said Deepa. 'I've heard stories about girls having secret love affairs with film producers and directors – even the ugly ones – just to get a break. Some aspects of this business are so seedy... it's definitely not all it's cracked up to be.'

'Come on, Deepa, don't be so down about it,' urged Amrita. 'You're really lucky to be such a star. Don't underestimate what you have. You'd regret it if it all just disappeared.'

'But what do I do about tonight?'

'Like I said, if I were you, I'd do my best to avoid it,' said the stylist in no uncertain terms. 'Fake an illness or something.'

Deepa looked at Amrita with a worried expression. Could she really do that? Wouldn't Vijay be furious? Her stomach turned over, and as she went to face the camera all she could think about was how she was going to avoid being alone with her lecherous film director.

* * *

After the crew had dined in the hotel restaurant that evening, Deepa called down to reception and asked the telephone operator to phone Vijay Kaul and tell him she was feeling sick and was therefore unable to see him.

It wasn't far from the truth either. The stress of this situation had almost made Deepa sick.

'What's wrong, *beti*,' asked Shanta, realising all was not right.

'Nothing, Mum. Just a stomach ache, I'll be fine in the morning,' Deepa mumbled from under her duvet.

It was most unlike Deepa to go to sleep so early as she always sat up in bed and read or watched TV, so Shanta was concerned. As was Ajay.

He had been calling her mobile but because Deepa wasn't sure that she'd sound convincing on the phone, she'd sent him a text message. It read:

`'Feel a bit odd, early night will sort me out. Deepa, X'`

She didn't want to lie to Ajay but felt it was okay to use that line. After all, she did feel 'odd' taking such extreme measures just to get out of a meeting. The whole thing kept playing on her mind, so in an effort to block it all out Deepa closed her eyes and forced herself to sleep.

By eight o'clock the following morning, most of the crew members were hungrily tucking into a delicious breakfast.

Deepa was still in the queue, though. She'd ordered an omelette, which the chef was cooking up in front of her. As she waited, Vijay sidled up to her. 'All you had to say was "no",' he whispered so that nobody else could hear. 'I'd have respected you more for it. Lying about being ill and then prancing around with commoners outside the hotel was not the cleverest thing to do.'

Deepa was stunned. She didn't even turn to look at him. She just stared at the chef as he tossed the omelette up in the air. How did Vijay know she'd faked her illness? And what did he mean about her dancing with commoners? For the second time in two days Deepa had no words for Vijay Kaul. She just wanted the ground to swallow her up.

Vijay grabbed a croissant, a pot of butter and a cup of tea and headed towards a table to the rear of the restaurant. Once Deepa had her breakfast tray in her hand, she looked around for Amrita.

Her make-up artist was sitting alone reading a newspaper, and Deepa rushed over to join her while her bodyguard, Aman, stood to one side and kept a watchful eye over her.

'Oh my God, Amrita,' Deepa whispered to the girl who was fast becoming her best friend and confidante. 'Things just go from bad to worse. I want to go home.'

She cupped her face in her hands.

'What happened?' Amrita asked in a whisper, folding up her paper and putting it aside. 'Did you blag an illness? Did he buy it?'

'Yes,' said Deepa plainly. She took a deep breath. 'And, no, he didn't buy it. He said I could have just said no instead of lying about being ill. And then he said something about dancing outside the hotel with commoners. What the hell does that mean? I tell you, either I'm going mad or it's everyone else.'

'Well at least you know for sure what he had in mind for last night, or he wouldn't have been so offended. Dirty creep,' she said in disgust as she looked around the restaurant for him. 'There he is, sad case.'

'Don't look at him, Amrita!' Deepa ordered. 'Or he'll know we're talking about him.'

'So? He should know. Oh look,' Amrita then said, pointing at the entrance. 'It's your mum with her son-in-law.'

Deepa turned around. 'Oh stop it!' she laughed. 'Maybe one day, but it's not likely right now. I'd better go and find a table for them,' Deepa added. 'Sorry to burden you with all this, but it's just so weird and I don't feel I can tell either of them.'

'Yeah, it's all a bit sordid isn't it?'

'You can say that again! Me and Ajay have just

about got things sorted, and now I've stressed him out about this stalker. He doesn't need me going on about directors trying to lure me into their hotel rooms as well.'

'No worries. Don't stress about it, Deepa. See you later.'

Deepa went to join her mum and Ajay, and as the three of them sat down to have breakfast together she felt her mobile phone vibrating in her bag. She took it out and looked at the display. It flashed: 'Simran'.

'Hi, Deepa, can you talk?' asked Simran, a freelance agent who was trying to get Deepa some work.

'Yes, sure, just having breakfast in Goa.'

'Okay, I won't be long,' Simran replied. 'I just wanted to tell you I think I've got a brilliant project for you. Produced by Big Banner Productions and co-starring Marc Fernandez.'

'Cool,' smiled Deepa. She knew her dad would be really chuffed about this one. Both the hero and production company were very well respected.

'You'll have a double role in the film. I'll get the script sent to your house ready for your return but there would a month-long shoot overseas in October. Are you up for it in principle?'

'Yeah,' enthused Deepa. 'Sounds really good. Who's directing it?'

'Oh sorry,' replied Simran. 'Forgot to tell you the most important part. It's Vijay Kaul. You're obviously doing all the right things in Goa at the moment,' added Simran, unaware that she had just wiped the smile from Deepa's face. 'It was Vijay who called to tell me they're on the lookout for a heroine. Seems like he's really taken to you.'

Chapter 8

Ajay stood on the balcony of his hotel later that evening, enjoying a cool lemon drink and looking at the beautiful Goan beach laid out in front of him. He was contemplating whether to give Deepa a call to see if she'd go out to dinner with him, but was hesitant to ask because he wasn't sure how her mum would feel about it.

'Damned stalker,' he thought to himself. If it hadn't been for the security issue, perhaps Deepa would have come to Goa alone and they could have managed to spend some quality time together.

Just as he was mulling all this over in his head, Ajay suddenly spotted the lady in question. She was standing amongst some bushes below, a few feet away from the balcony. His face lit up.

'Hey, Deepa. What are you doing there?'

She looked up at him and smiled.

'Why are you so dressed up? Are you going out?' Ajay asked, trying to keep his voice down so any passers-by wouldn't hear.

She shook her head.

'Why don't you come up and have a drink with me, then?'

'Later.' She looked around and seemed to wave at someone before glancing back up at Ajay. She gave him a long, lingering gaze, a flying kiss and then ran off.

'Funny girl,' said Ajay to himself, perplexed. 'What does she mean by that?'

He made his way back inside and decided to watch some TV while he waited for Deepa to call. Hopefully, they would still have time to meet after she had finished whatever it was she was doing.

Two hours later, though, there was no sign of Deepa and Ajay decided to go to her hotel room to see what was happening. He stood outside, paused, and then knocked softly. It was a few moments before the door opened. Shanta greeted him.

'Aah, *namaste* Auntiji, how are you?'

'Fine, *beta* – just waiting for Deepa to come back and then I can get some sleep.'

'Oh? She's not back? Did she say where she was going?'

'Some last-minute rehearsal, apparently. Everyone got a phone call. Why aren't you there?'

'I don't know anything about it,' he replied. 'Where is it?'

'I'm not sure. Around the hotel complex somewhere. I didn't think to ask.'

Ajay's eyes widened in horror. 'Auntiji, there's no rehearsal that I know of. I saw Deepa downstairs a couple of hours ago. Outside the hotel.'

'A couple of hours? No, you couldn't have,' said Shanta. 'She only left half an hour ago. Before that she was here all evening.'

Ajay furrowed his brow and his expression turned to one of concern.

'Do you know who called her?'

'No. She didn't say,' replied Shanta.

'Listen, as far as I know, there are no rehearsals this evening. She shouldn't have gone out alone – what if the phone call was made by the stalker? Has the security guard gone with her?'

'Oh my God! What are you saying?' Shanta screeched, covering her mouth with her hand. 'I didn't even think about that! I don't know if she's got Aman with her or not. He's usually stationed outside the room. If he's not there now he must be with Deepa. Come, *beta*, we have to find her!'

Shanta was wearing her towelling hotel robe and had rollers in her hair, but she didn't care. She hurriedly put her flip-flops on and grabbed hold of Ajay's hand. The security guard was nowhere to be seen, so Ajay dialled Deepa's mobile phone number but there was no reply. The pair then marched to the lift. Ajay pressed a button to take them down one floor. Once the doors opened, he rushed out and ran up the corridor. He knocked rapidly on Vikram's door.

'What's wrong?' asked Vikram when he saw Ajay and Shanta standing in the doorway. He was rubbing his eyes and looked as though he'd been sleeping.

'Has Deepa got some kind of rehearsal tonight?' Ajay asked, anxiety almost choking his voice. 'Apparently she received a phone call in her room and was called for a rehearsal, but Aunt*ji* doesn't know who she's with or where she's gone.'

Vikram yawned. 'Nope, there's nothing as far as I

know, unless it's a beauty or stylist thing. Ask Amrita.'

Ajay hurriedly dialled Amrita's number on his mobile while Shanta stood with her hands clasped together, praying for the safe return of her daughter.

'Amrita, is Deepa with you?'

'Erm, nope. Why? I thought she was spending the evening in her room.'

'She's out, some rehearsal apparently, but we can't work out who with. Sorry, got to go. Bye.'

'Damn!' snapped Ajay as he slammed his phone shut. 'Vikram, call hotel security and find out where Aman is,' he ordered. 'We don't know where Deepa's gone and you're saying there are no rehearsals, so this is really worrying. We're gonna go and check out the reception areas downstairs.'

On his way to the lift, Ajay dialled Deepa's mobile number again. This time it went straight to voicemail.

'Oh, I can't walk any more,' cried Shanta as she raised her hands to her chest and panted for breath. 'I should have gone with her! Oh my poor Deepa!'

'Auntiji, it's not your fault,' said Ajay, hammering the lift button a good few times even though it was already lit up. 'Try to calm down and conserve your energy for finding her. We need to think clearly.' The lift seemed to be taking for ever so Ajay decided to run down the stairs and told Shanta to meet him by the reception desk.

'Have you seen Miss Deepa Khanna?' Ajay asked the receptionist on duty. She shook her head. 'Find her security guard's mobile number – fast! I'm just gonna check around here.'

Ajay ran into one of the big meeting rooms by the lobby area. It was empty. Then, thinking she may have been called for a last-minute dance rehearsal, he tried the big hall adjacent to it. There was nobody there, either.

By now Ajay was beginning to panic. He ran back to Reception and was just about to ask them to call the police when he caught sight of a couple sitting in a booth, tucked away at the back of the hotel bar.

Ajay ran towards the pair and felt relief flood through his body as he finally saw Deepa. She was with the director, Vijay Kaul.

'Oh my God, Deepa!' Ajay exclaimed as he reached their table. He leaned on it and took a few deep breaths. 'We were so worried–' Ajay suddenly stopped in mid-sentence. He was sure he'd just seen Vijay snatch his hand away from Deepa's knee.

Vijay seemed to sense that Ajay had spotted him and started rubbing his hands nervously.

'What's wrong, Ajay?' asked Deepa, looking slightly uncomfortable herself. 'You said you were worried. About what?'

'Oh… nothing. Your mum was looking for you, that's all.'

'That's strange,' commented Vijay. 'I thought that Deepa told her she was attending a meeting. But anyway, Ajay, I'm glad you came,' he added, obviously lying. 'I was just running through some things with Deepa… A little tutorial on authentic facial expressions in romantic scenes. Please join us. A drink?'

Ajay looked at Vijay and then again at Deepa, who still looked very edgy.

'I have to run back and find your mum, Deepa. She was a bit concerned as she didn't know if the guard was with you or not. She's walking around the hotel searching for you now. Where is Aman?'

Deepa pointed to a corner of the bar, where the security guard was sitting with a Coke in his hand. 'I'll come with you,' she said, easing out of the booth. 'I told Mum I was rehearsing. I can't believe she's running around looking for me!'

'Yeah, long story,' muttered Ajay, very perturbed by what he had just seen. 'Let's find her and put her mind at rest first.'

'Sorry, Vijay *sahib*, this is a bit embarrassing, but I better go and see that Mum's okay.'

'Don't worry, Deepa,' Vijay replied, taking a sip of his whisky and ice. 'No problem. We can do this some other time. Bye.'

Ajay and Deepa rushed to Reception and Aman followed closely behind. They found Shanta leaning against the desk as though she was trying to prop herself up. She looked frantic with worry.

'Oh, Mum! Look at you! I told you I was in the hotel, why did you freak out? You look like you're gonna collapse!'

Shanta couldn't get any words out, but tears streamed down her cheeks as she hugged her daughter. Ajay stood behind the pair, and once Shanta had managed to get some control over her emotions somewhat he suggested they all go back to their rooms.

'You idiot guard!' Shanta yelled at Aman. 'We've been trying to call your mobile! Why is it switched off?'

Aman felt around in his shirt pocket and apologised as he explained that he must have left the phone in his room.

'Call yourself top film star security!' Shanta spewed out. 'You're a village bumpkin, that's what you are! You're not fit for the job!'

Aman looked acutely embarrassed but Ajay grabbed hold of Shanta's hand and led her back towards her room. Once Aman had resumed his position outside the door, Deepa and Ajay took Shanta inside and sat her down on the bed.

'Rest, Aunti*ji*. I'm sorry for all this,' said Ajay. 'If I hadn't come up, none of it would have happened.'

'It's okay, *beta*,' said Shanta. 'Thanks for being with us. It's really hard, you know – two women staying in a hotel without the man of the house. I know we mock Deepa's father – he's a difficult man at the best of times – but he protects us. I've never felt so vulnerable before.'

Ajay hugged Shanta to reassure her that he was there for them, and Deepa then followed him to the door.

'I'm glad you came when you did,' Deepa told him. 'Thanks for looking out for me.'

Ajay turned his back and started to walk off. He took a few steps then looked back at Deepa. 'If you hadn't told me you'd meet me later when I was on the balcony, I'd never have gone looking for you. But I was waiting for you for hours,' he said. 'Look, it's probably not my place to say this,' continued Ajay, downbeat, 'but be wary of Vijay. He's well known for his private "tutorials" with starlets. Nobody else got called for a rehearsal tonight. I'd question his motives, if I were you. Look after your mum; I'll see you in the morning.'

He headed off down the corridor. Deepa watched as he disappeared around the corner. Ajay was right about Vijay's motives. Vijay had told her on the phone that the crew were doing a late rehearsal and she had to come. When she got there, though, he changed his story and told her he needed only her because she needed to focus on emotional expression.

Vijay's intentions were suspect, that was clear. But what wasn't quite so clear was what Ajay meant when he said he'd talked to her from his balcony and that she'd arranged to meet him later that evening.

She had never seen Ajay on the balcony.

* * *

The following day's schedule was very intense. They shot most of the beach song sequence, and after several hours, Deepa was happy to get a break from filming and just roam around like a tourist for a while. She was enjoying her work, but didn't like the fact that she couldn't go anywhere without Aman. She was also frustrated that things between her and

Ajay were not really going in the direction she'd hoped.

'He's not just good looking, he's kind too,' Deepa smiled as she strolled through the street market with Amrita. Aman ambled a few steps behind. 'But it doesn't seem like we're gonna get any time alone on this trip.'

'I'll bet,' said Amrita. 'When you've got creeps like Vijay Kaul tricking you into meeting them, there's not much chance of anything developing with Ajay, is there?'

Deepa nodded. 'Yeah, that was bad, but Ajay saved me. Vijay had his hand on my knee when Ajay got there... I didn't know what to do. Talk about timing!'

The two girls strode on at a leisurely pace, chatting and admiring the goods on show at the same time. There were pretty wooden trinkets, silver jewellery and handpainted mughal art paintings on offer, but Deepa knew they were aimed at the huge number of foreign tourists that visited Goa. No Indian would pay the prices the tradesmen asked for.

'Prices here must be inflated by three hundred per cent, don't you reckon, Amrita?' asked Deepa.

'At least,' she mused. 'But everything is so gorgeous and in this peaceful environment, who wouldn't fall for it? I may take a few pieces home myself – after haggling the prices down though.'

Checking out a few beautifully crafted ornaments, Amrita stopped at a stall to discuss the price of a tall, handpainted vase. Deepa decided to wait under the shelter of an empty stall opposite as the sun was so bright. She could feel her shoulders beginning to burn and wished she'd worn something over her cap-sleeved top to cover her arms.

The market had suddenly become very busy as groups of excited shoppers came out looking for bargains before returning to their hotels in time for lunch. Deepa was idly watching them go by when there was a tap on her shoulder.

'Yeah?' said Deepa turning around. She expected it to be Amrita or Aman. It was neither.

'*Aaaaaarggghhhhh*!' she screamed.

Panic set in. 'Amrita! *Help*! He's here! He's here! THE STALKER!'

Deepa wanted to run but she was gripped by fear and didn't know which way to turn.

It was a few seconds before Aman realised what was happening, and in those short moments the man fled and managed to lose himself in the crowd.

Aman ran through the groups of shoppers, pushing them carelessly aside as he went searching for his target. He hadn't got a good look at the man and wasn't sure who he was chasing, but he had to try because his neck would be on the line for getting sidetracked from his duty. It was no good, though. The stalker had vanished.

Deepa was sobbing in Amrita's arms when Aman returned, empty-handed. 'I want to go home,' she cried, wiping away the tears that had made her mascara run down her face.

People all around had been alerted by Deepa's cries, and now they began to realise who she was. A crowd quickly gathered so Aman put his arms protectively around both girls, hailed the first yellow taxi he saw and took them back to the hotel.

'Come on, Deepa. Let's get you inside,' said Amrita, with her arm tightly around her friend's waist. Followed closely by Aman, Amrita took Deepa straight up to her room. When Shanta opened the door Deepa broke free of Amrita's grip and rushed straight into her mother's arms, sobbing loudly.

'What's wrong, Deepa?' asked Shanta, alarmed.

Deepa couldn't get any words out, so Amrita explained what had happened.

'Foolish security man!' scolded Shanta. 'Are you hired by the police to look after my daughter or to shop around for market bargains? I'm calling your boss at once. I told you, you're not up to the job!'

Aman hung his head. He knew he had made a bad mistake.

The police inspector was summoned and Aman was told he would be placed elsewhere for failing to carry out his duties satisfactorily. As a result, Deepa was assigned two new security guards, but she still wasn't happy.

'I want to go home, Mum. This trip has been a disaster,' she said when they were alone in their room later that night.

'No, we can't go Deepa,' Shanta said. 'You need to finish the film or your dad will go mad. Not a word of any of this to him, okay?'

'But why?' Deepa asked, feeling distraught. 'It's not my fault. It's his fault we're here anyway. I keep telling him I don't think I'm cut out for this. I want a simple life,' said Deepa, tears welling up in her eyes again. 'I'm being followed, I can't go anywhere, our hotel room has been broken into, I'm accused of being in odd places, doing things I haven't even done… this is too much for anyone, especially a shy seventeen-year-old like me!'

'Deepa, be rational, *beti*. Don't make rash decisions,' said Shanta, taking a seat next to her on the bed. 'Maybe there's an innocent explanation for all of this.'

'Innocent? A man has followed me all the way from Mumbai to Goa and it's got to the point where he has the nerve to approach me – he even touched my shoulder! Are you guys only going to take this seriously when I've been kidnapped or something? Is that what it's going to take?'

Shanta sat with her head bowed down. She had no answer.

The silence was broken by a knock on the door.

'It's Vijay Kaul here.'

Shanta peered through the peephole to double check and then let him in. He had heard all about the incident in the market and had a plan. 'Deepa, you're free to go home the day after tomorrow. I've had a word with the producer on the phone and with Vikram, and we all agree you need to go.'

'What about the rest of the shoot?' Deepa asked, looking up at him.

'We just need to can a few more shots for the song. We can do that tomorrow and maybe the morning after if need be,' he proposed. 'But we'll have to start early tomorrow. You'll need to be up and out by seven o'clock.'

Deepa nodded.

'The other scenes are mainly Ajay's,' continued Vijay. 'There is one scene we need you for, but it's an indoor shot. If we don't get time for it, we can shoot it in a Mumbai studio.'

Deepa smiled in acceptance of his offer. She was desperate to get back to Mumbai.

The following morning the crew headed back to the beach and completed a few more segments of the song. The remaining scenes were canned the morning after, and by five o'clock that day Deepa was packed and ready to go home.

With her new security men in tow, Deepa and Shanta said their goodbyes to the cast and crew. Because they were leaving at such short notice they had been unable to find a flight home, so had to settle for Vikram's offer of a private car back to Mumbai.

Deepa didn't mind as she just wanted to go home where she felt a bit safer. Shanta, on the other hand, wasn't at all pleased. 'I'm sure they could have got us seats in first class but that tight-fisted Vikram probably didn't want to,' she moaned as the car pulled away from the Indian Heritage Hotel.

Deepa turned around and looked through the rear window. She could see Ajay standing alongside everyone, waving goodbye.

This is not how she had hoped her Goan adventure would end. She tried to hide her sadness from her mother, but as Shanta continued complaining, Deepa grabbed a tissue from her handbag and dabbed tears away from her eyes.

'I wish I'd been at the market with you,' said Shanta when she realised Deepa wasn't about to join her in berating Vikram. 'I would have beaten the man to a pulp myself. Following you all the way from Mumbai, he's got a nerve!'

Shanta turned to look at Deepa, but seeing her daughter was quite upset she quickly changed her tune. 'Don't worry, *beti*. These things happen. Maybe it's just God's way of telling us that you're going to be such a huge star, and that we need to come to terms with it now.'

Deepa wasn't convinced and didn't want to discuss it any more. She turned to look out of the window and watched as the beautiful red sun slowly dipped behind the palm tree-lined street.

'Look on the bright side, Deepa,' continued Shanta. 'We should be glad all this happened in Goa and not Mumbai. Can you imagine dealing with this and the media on top of that? At least we don't have to worry about being in the papers.'

But Shanta had no idea how wrong she was.

In the early hours of the morning, when they pulled up outside their home, both women were shocked to see what looked like the whole world's press and television crews camped outside.

'Oh my God! Has something happened to Sachin or your dad?' panicked Shanta. 'What's happening, Deepa? Find out.'

Flanked by her security men, Deepa ran out of the car and, keeping her head down, dashed to the front of the house. The reporters were calling her, all asking questions. One voice stood out from the rest. It shouted, 'Deepa Khanna, what made you do it?'

Deepa hastily opened the front door of the house and was relieved to see her brother and dad alive and well, albeit stressed, sitting on the sofa, staring at the television.

'*Didi!*' cried Sachin as soon as he saw Deepa. He jumped up and gave her a big hug. Shanta ran in behind her.

'What's going on?' she screeched. 'Sachin *beta*, are you ok?' She grabbed her son and kissed him on the head.

'Dad, what's happened?' asked Deepa. She was actually frightened of hearing his reply but needed to know.

'Sit down, Deepa,' he replied softly. Deepa had

never heard her father speak so gently. She knew it must be bad.

Jayant coughed.

'Tell me, Dad. What's wrong? Is it the stalker?'

'No,' Jayant began. 'The police were here two hours ago.'

'Police?' asked Deepa.

Her dad nodded. He looked weary as though he was also finding things difficult to deal with.

'I know it's not you, but they think it is.'

'What's not me?' asked Deepa frustrated with her dad for not getting to the point. 'Sachin, you tell me,' she urged her kid brother, who was clinging to Shanta.

'They say they have camera footage of you stealing from a clothes shop in Goa,' said Sachin. 'Last night.'

'What?' Deepa asked, her eyes widening in confusion. 'Is that it?' She heaved a huge sigh of relief and slumped on the sofa. 'I thought something really awful had happened,' she laughed.

Nobody laughed with her.

'They'll have to take you to the station for questioning. It's very embarrassing,' said Jayant.

'Why?' Deepa challenged. 'It's obviously a mistake. I wasn't even in Goa last night. We left at five o'clock that day, it's ridiculous! It's impossible!'

'Yes, but the police say they have photos to prove it, and even though I know it's not you it's still going to take time to clear your name.'

Deepa was gobsmacked. She didn't know what to say and couldn't understand why her dad wasn't hopping mad at the police for having the gall to accuse her, knowing she was innocent.

Shanta also just stood there in silence.

'Mum, can you say something, please?' said Deepa, irritated. 'You were with me in that bloody car all last night, for God's sake! You know it's not me, don't you?'

Shanta nodded but then burst into tears and slumped into a chair, sobbing into a crumpled corner of her saree.

Deepa couldn't get to grips with what was happening around her. She should have been on a high now that her career was in full flight, but somehow things kept going wrong. And what was really strange was her dad's subdued reaction to all this. Normally he went into full rant mode at the slightest thing.

Just as she was contemplating whether she should go outside and take on the journalists herself, there was a knock on the door. Deepa rushed to open it.

'Deepa, come back!' ordered Jayant. But it was too late. She had already opened the door and was shocked to see two police officers outside. Flashbulbs popped and photographers hungrily snapped away, trying to get a shot that could earn them the equivalent of a year's wages.

'We need to take you to the station for questioning about some alleged thefts,' began one of the policemen.

'Thefts? Is it more than one now? And you actually believe I'm a thief?' Deepa shouted.

She turned around and saw her mum, dad and brother watching helplessly as the police officers escorted her down the path and into their waiting car. There were more policemen outside the gate of the house, trying to control the eager photographers.

Deepa's emotions as she got into the police car were a heightened mix of anger, humiliation and sadness. But through all of that came the sudden realisation that all these odd sightings of her were no coincidence. There was somebody out there pretending to be her, and more than anything else Deepa wanted to find out who that person was.

Chapter 9

Deepa couldn't believe her eyes. She could see how anyone watching this footage of a young girl neatly lifting designer clothes from the rails of a top boutique and slipping them into her bag would think it was her.

'Oh my God!' Deepa said to the policewoman who was showing her the clip. 'That looks EXACTLY like me! It's so much like me,' she continued in amazement. Deepa moved closer and studied a freeze-frame of the girl's face. 'But still, it should be obvious that it's not me.'

The police officer shot a look at Deepa that suggested she was mad.

'Don't believe me? Then look!' exclaimed Deepa. 'Forget the fact that her hair is slightly shorter than mine – I could be wearing hair extensions for argument's sake – but look…'

She pointed to the screen.

'There's no beauty spot there above her lip, it's clear enough to see that!'

The policewoman focused on where Deepa was pointing and then turned to look at a male officer who was standing behind.

'Yes, Madam,' he began, moving closer to Deepa. 'We hear what you say, but it's only CCTV footage – it doesn't pick up all the detail.'

'And make-up can easily disguise a beauty spot,' added the female officer.

'Oh well, why don't you just arrest me and charge me, then?' said Deepa, folding her arms in frustration. 'But how could it be me?' she insisted, waving her hands around. 'I was in a taxi with my mum and two security guards, driving back from Goa. The guards are still at my house. You can check with them!'

'We will do everything we need to, Ma'am, I assure you,' said the policeman.

'It's all a ploy! A man has been following me

around for weeks and people keep saying they've seen me in places where I haven't been,' explained Deepa. 'Something's obviously going on! These people must be part of a gang and they're using me to hide their crimes or something… They've clearly found a good lookalike.'

'That's more than a lookalike, Madam. It's a carbon copy,' said the female officer.

'I agree! But mega-famous superstars often have people impersonating them, don't they? I saw this programme about a Michael Jackson lookalike and he was always getting chased around wherever he went when Michael Jackson was alive because people thought he really was Michael. Maybe this girl has had plastic surgery to look like me – it's not that far-fetched, is it? Anything is possible these days.'

The officers kept quiet. They didn't know quite how to answer that one, so they just nodded and assured Deepa they'd check out her alibi.

They asked Deepa to wait while they filed some paperwork and then called her family to inform them she was ready to come home.

The time Deepa spent sitting alone in the police station felt like the lowest point of her life. She didn't even want to look up at anyone. It was awful to be accused of stealing and even worse that they all seemed to have decided she was guilty. She couldn't even bear to think about the feeding frenzy the press would have over the photos of her being led away by the police.

When her dad arrived, Deepa ran up to him and hugged him tightly. He kissed her forehead and held her for a long time. She looked up and was surprised to see tears in his eyes.

It was a strange, surreal journey back home. Deepa sat next to her dad in the back seat but neither said a word. Instead, they clutched hands tightly, silently letting each other know they would get through this together.

Shanta was waiting up for them when they got back, but Sachin had gone to bed. Her mum's puffy eyes told Deepa she had spent the evening crying.

Deepa took Shanta's hands in hers. 'Don't worry, Mum,' she said boldly, trying to make out everything was under control. 'I spoke to the police and they said it's possible an imposter is posing as me. There could even be a whole gang behind this. They'll catch the person – or people – soon.'

Shanta gave Deepa a hug, but then started sobbing again. She broke away from her daughter and ran off into the kitchen, not wanting to upset her any further. It broke Deepa's heart to see her mum like this.

Deepa's two security guards took up their positions – one at the back of the house and one at the front – and Deepa went upstairs to her room. She took a few deep breaths. She was feeling claustrophobic and needed some air to clear her head so she opened the double doors that led to her private balcony.

She stepped outside, closed her eyes and took a deep breath in. As she opened her eyes again, she looked down to the garden.

Her heart started pounding at what she saw.

It was dark, but there was no mistaking who was standing there, looking up at her.

Deepa screamed as hard as she could and it wasn't long before the security guards rushed into the garden, grabbing the man and grappling him to the ground. As all the security lights came on in the garden, Deepa could see the intruder lying on his back in the middle of the lawn. He looked shocked, like a rabbit caught in headlights.

Deepa covered her face with her hands, then peeked through the gaps in her fingers.

'What happened, *beti*? What happened? Are you all right?' shouted Jayant as he rushed into her bedroom and out on to the balcony. Shanta scuttled in after him.

Deepa was as pale as a sheet and she buried her face in her mum's bosom.

As the guards began leading the man away, far out of sight, his voice finally reached Deepa.

'Dimple!' he called out.

She started, then looked at her mum and dad in confusion.

'Dimple!' he cried again.

Jayant and Shanta exchanged worried glances.

'How does he know my real name is Dimple?' asked Deepa.

Again, she looked at her mum and dad for an answer. They looked away.

'Nobody knows I was called Dimple when I was born. You never told anyone that you changed the name later. How could he have found that out?'

There was silence.

Deepa moved right to the front of the balcony and watched as the man was forcefully led away by the guards. As the man was removed from Deepa's sight, his anguished cries began to fade. Deepa once again turned to look at her parents. Both of them were standing with their heads bowed down. Her father had clasped his hands together and was shaking his head. It was all too much for him and he took a seat on the edge of Deepa's bed.

'He called me Dimple,' said Deepa. 'Dimple!'

Shanta and Jayant still didn't comment.

'Do you know this man?' asked Deepa, pointing at her dad. Her brain began to rewind the events of the past few weeks as she attempted to make sense of the many incomprehensible things that had happened.

Jayant sighed. 'Tell her now, Shanta. It's not fair. She'll hear it from the newspapers if you don't tell her first.'

'Tell me what?' asked Deepa incredulously. 'You do know this man, don't you?'

'Well, it's not quite like that,' began Shanta.

'Not quite like what? I've been worried sick about a stalker and now you're telling me you know who he is? Mum! You were in Goa with me, watching me go through hell, and you knew the man all along!'

'You've got it wrong, *beti*!' Shanta cried out. 'I thought there was a stalker too. I never saw the man who was following you when you did your photo shoot or when he turned up in the market in Goa. I really thought someone might be trying to harm you… I had no idea he would turn out to be your grandfather!'

Shanta burst into tears.

'Grandfather?' Deepa sat down. She clutched at the bedsheets with both her hands. The anger had gone. Shock took its place.

'That man being led away by security guards is my grandfather? As in Dad's dad? You told me I didn't have any grandparents on dad's side–' She suddenly stopped.

'Am I adopted?' Her heart sank. 'Who am I?' she screamed. It was too much for her, she no longer knew who or what to believe.

'No, no darling,' said her dad, moving closer and putting his arm around her. Deepa tightened up. She wasn't feeling affectionate right now.

'We are your real parents,' he explained. 'We just haven't told you everything about your life.'

Deepa listened, aghast.

'You have a grandfather you don't know about,' Jayant began. 'My mum died when I was young, but that man downstairs is my father, Shankar.'

Tears rolled freely down her dad's face as he told her the truth he'd kept from her for so long.

'My father had two sons,' he began. 'We got married within a year of each other and all lived happily together in Goa... until I messed up.'

'Goa?' mumbled Deepa. She was trying to put

the pieces of this crazy jigsaw together.

'I… urm… got into some financial difficulties after an insane night of gambling and, without telling my dad or brother, sold off some family land by faking their signatures.

'I was scared because I was being threatened by the person who won the bet,' he continued, hanging his head in shame. 'He was a local gangster and he would have beaten me to a pulp – or worse – if I didn't come up with the money. That was the only way I thought I could do it.'

Deepa could barely believe her ears. Shanta sobbed in the background.

'As you'd expect, my father and brother were furious. They disowned me. Told me to leave.'

'And we had to leave my baby behind!' Shanta blubbed loudly.

'What?' asked Deepa. 'Me?'

'No, Neha… your sister… your twin,' she replied. 'I think about her every day. What a punishment for a mother! It must be my bad karma, something bad I have done in a previous life.'

Deepa stood still. All of a sudden, everything clicked into place. The angry young man at Javed's Audio Visual Cave who was convinced he'd had a relationship with Deepa… the sighting of Deepa out on the town with a strange man… the visions of Deepa outside the Goan hotel… and most tragically, the theft.

'That girl… is my twin?'

Deepa put her head in her hands and started to cry with huge, heart-rending sobs. Shanta pursed her lips, trying to contain her own emotions and Jayant felt as though his heart would break. He reached out to Deepa, trying to offer her comfort.

'Go away!' she screamed.

'*Beti*, please let us expl–'

'GO AWAY! I don't want any more explanations from you two liars!'

'Deepa, we know you're upset–'

'No! Don't talk to me!' Deepa screamed wildly, running out of the room and rushing down the stairs. 'This is your house! You stay. I'M GOING!'

'But where will you go in the middle of the night?' asked Jayant. 'Please think, Deepa.'

The suitcase that Deepa had brought back from Goa was still sitting by the front door. She grabbed it along with her handbag and raced out of the front door, slamming it shut behind her.

'Deepa!' her mum screamed from inside the house. 'Come back!'

'Let her go, Shanta,' sobbed Jayant, pulling his

wife back. 'Let her go. This is our fault… my fault. She needs to be alone. Let her go.'

Deepa could hear her parents weeping inside the house but she felt no sympathy for them. All her life she had tried to please her father and he had played the cruellest trick of all. He had separated her from her twin and then lied about it for seventeen years.

The journalists had gone now and Deepa walked a few steps down the path before a security guard came running up to her. 'Is everything all right Ma'am? We called the police. He's been taken away.'

'Please take me to…' she stopped. Both Ajay and Amrita were still in Goa – they weren't due back for two more days. She couldn't believe her bad luck. 'This could only happen to me,' she said sadly. 'I've left home but with nowhere to go.'

She fought back the tears but walked over to the security guard's car.

'Where do you want to go, Madam? I'll take you.'

'Thanks,' said Deepa. 'I don't know the address, but I can give you directions. I want to go to Bela's house, please.'

* * *

It was quite a job getting past the security at Bela's residence, and once she was through, Deepa felt she would drop from sheer exhaustion. But she knew she still had to make it up to her fellow actress and then ask whether she could stay for a day or two until she sorted herself out.

'Deepa!' said Bela, looking very surprised as she opened the door. 'The guard said it was you and I told him it couldn't be. Sorry if you had trouble getting in, it's just that it's so late. Are you okay?'

Deepa shook her head. Tears streamed down her cheeks.

'Oh my goodness!' said Bela, looking concerned. 'Come in.'

Deepa stepped inside and Bela took her straight to the living room. 'My parents are away, so please feel relaxed,' she said, gently touching Deepa's arm. 'Sit down. Now tell me what's wrong.'

When Deepa could finally stop crying and managed to get some words out she filled Bela in on everything that had happened.

'Oh my goodness!' exclaimed Bela. 'I knew it was you at the party… well, you know what I mean! I didn't know what was going on when you accused me of lying the next day, I kept going over it in my head and I was sure I'd seen your face. I couldn't understand how you were behaving that evening, failing to recognise people and being so different…

I just put it down to the success going to your head.'

'What success?' Deepa asked in bewilderment. 'I'm not a success like you. It's all a complete mess.' She shook her head. 'I thought being an actress was going to be about dressing up in nice clothes and singing great songs. There's a lot more to this business than I can handle… It's really not for me.'

'Don't say that, Deepa,' said Bela kindly, taking her hand in hers. 'Of course it's for you. People think movie stars have an easy life, but they don't. I found it really hard at first too, but you get used to it. People loved you in *Mumbai Magic*. You have to carry on.'

Deepa raised a faint smile, touched by Bela's compliment. 'You're being so kind to me. Aren't you angry with me for that row? I was pretty mean to you. I'm sorry.'

'Don't be silly. It wasn't you at the party so of course you were going to be angry – I should be the one apologising!' replied Bela. 'But your sister is identical to you, except for the curly hair.'

'Really?' Deepa suddenly found herself wanting to know all about her sibling. 'Is she taller than me? Thinner?'

'She's *exactly* like you,' said Bela. 'It's funny that you should be asking me about your twin! Why don't you try to meet her? Find out where she lives and go and see her.'

Deepa's eyes welled up again. 'My sister is a thief,' she blurted out.

'What?'

Deepa began to tell Bela all about the theft incident. Bela listened intently and then said, 'I don't have all the answers, Deepa, but I do think you have to give your sister a fair hearing. This is a lot for anyone to take in and you're obviously upset just now with your parents. Find out why all these things happened, but only when you're ready,' she advised. 'First, don't you think you need to go and see if your grandfather is okay?'

Deepa nodded.

'Do you want to go to the police station right now? I'll come with you if you like.'

'Yes… please.'

'Okay, give me a few minutes to get changed. I'll call my driver and we'll be out in fifteen minutes.'

Deepa didn't really feel ready to face the situation yet – just two hours ago she'd thought this man was a stalker, and now she had discovered he was her long-deceased grandfather. But she knew Bela was right. They had to tell the police who he was and get him released.

Double Take

Once inside the local police station, Deepa asked for the chief inspector, and moments later she was sitting explaining all the bizarre goings-on to him.

'I see... so he IS your grandfather,' the chief inspector said. 'We didn't believe him. My officers are talking to him right now. Let me have a few words with them and we'll bring him out.'

The next few minutes seemed to last for ever. Bela stood supportively beside Deepa who was taking long, deep breaths trying to keep calm. Her stomach was churning.

'I don't know what to expect, Bela,' said Deepa. 'I'm angry, excited, and terrified all at the same time.'

'Of course you are,' smiled Bela, putting an arm lovingly around Deepa's shoulder. 'It's a mad situation... you're about to meet a grandfather you didn't even know about this morning. You're bound to be nervous.'

Deepa was trembling when, moments later, the man who she had feared was out to harm her finally appeared. He looked tired and worn, but as soon as he saw Deepa he reached out and gave her a huge, warm hug. Deepa was taken aback, but it felt so right, like the most natural thing in the world.

Bela took a few steps back to give the couple some space. It was such an emotional scene, even she had a few tears in her eyes. She reflected that she was unlikely to witness a reunion like this ever again, except on a film set. Fact, she thought to herself, is definitely stranger than fiction.

Once Deepa had signed some official paperwork at the station, Bela asked her driver, Raju, to take them back to her house. Although Shankar had been staying with a friend in Mumbai, Bela kindly offered him her guest room so he could spend some time getting to know Deepa.

Once they were back at the house, Bela asked her housemaid to organise the rooms while she went into the kitchen to make some coffee.

Shankar and Deepa took a seat in the living room.

'Dimple... oh sorry, Deepa... it's going to take time for me to get used to your new name.'

'That's okay,' said Deepa. 'I don't mind.'

'I've wanted to see you again for so many years, you know, but I had no idea where you were,' Shankar told her. 'It was only when you started appearing on film posters that I discovered you lived in Mumbai.'

'Why didn't you just try to talk to me all those times you came to see me?' Deepa asked, perplexed.

'I didn't know how to approach you,' explained

Shankar. 'I wasn't trying to harm you or scare you. I'm sorry you thought I was a stalker. You must have been terrified of me. I was devastated when I heard that,' he added, looking down and shaking his head in dismay.

'That day at the photo shoot, I was going to wait for you to finish your job, and then try to talk to you, but of course I got chased away. Then at the TV studio there were just too many people around.'

'It's such a shame,' said Deepa. 'It could have been so much easier than this. I feel awful for telling everyone there was a stalker after me. I had security guards with me in case you came back... they could have hurt you.'

'I wanted to talk to you in private, but I was never sure who else was with you. I didn't want your dad to know. We all fell out very badly,' Shankar revealed. 'Your dad did some silly things and his brother, my eldest son, was very angry. He wouldn't let your father stay in the house.' Shankar had a look of pain etched on his wrinkled face as he recalled how his happy family had split up.

'I'm so sorry,' said Deepa, feeling the need to apologise for her father's reckless behaviour.

'Don't be sorry Dimp... erm... erm... Deepa. How could you have known? You're an innocent victim in all of this mess.'

'But why did my sister stay behind? Why didn't she come with me and my parents? I don't understand why we were separated. It was so cruel.'

'It was, *beti*. It was,' acknowledged Shankar sadly. 'But your uncle didn't have any children of his own, and when this all happened you were just babies,' he recalled. 'Your father was leaving with nothing. He wouldn't have been able to support and raise both of you, so we felt the best thing to do was split you two up.'

Shankar stared ahead, lost in thought as he pondered that decision. It was clear he regretted it now.

'You were supposed to stay behind in Goa and Neha – your sister – was meant to go with your parents.'

Deepa was shocked.

'What?' She suddenly felt very unwanted and unloved.

'Yes, you were supposed to stay in Goa with us,' Shankar went on. 'But at the last moment, you got very sick with a chest infection. You kept crying and became very clingy. You wouldn't let anyone but your mother pick you up, so in the end you went with her and Neha stayed behind with us.'

He went silent for a moment. 'That is why Neha is so angry.'

'Angry?' Deepa looked quizzically at her grandfather as Bela walked into the room with three cups of steaming hot coffee.

'Yes,' nodded Shankar. 'It's why I came looking for you, and why I was so desperate to speak to you. She's trying to get back at you.'

'Huh? Get back at me for what?' Deepa was even more puzzled.

'Neha always knew she had a twin, we never kept it a secret from her, but she grew up resenting your father, blaming him for everything,' said Shankar. He stood up and walked to the far end of the room.

Then he turned to face Deepa and Bela, who were now seated next to each other holding their mugs of coffee. 'She considers your uncle to be her father. She's never let him feel he's not her real dad. Neha is a very tough girl and was reasonably content with her life… until you became a star.'

Deepa stared up at Shankar, trying to take it all in.

'When you became famous, though,' he continued, 'she started to feel angry. She began thinking she should have been the film star – that it should be her face up there on the billboards. Then she disappeared off to Mumbai, leaving a note to say she was going to 'sort a few things out'. I knew she was going to get up to mischief, so that's when I came looking for you.'

'Well, that explains a lot,' said Bela. 'Neha's been behaving badly in public places in Mumbai… dating guys… deliberately getting caught on CCTV stealing garments… all to get you in trouble!'

Deepa shook her head. 'How messed up is my life?' she asked sadly. 'A few hours ago, I didn't even know that I had a sister and now I'm discovering she hates me!'

'It's not her fault, *beti*,' said Shankar. Neha didn't grow up hating you. But I think she feels frustrated that she hasn't had the opportunities you've had. She's always been fascinated with the cinema and, even though we beg her not to, she goes to South Beach every day to perform songs and dances for the tourists. The locals know her as a '*banjaaran*' – gypsy girl – because of this. But she's not doing it for money. It's because she loves to entertain people.'

Deepa recalled the man at the Goan hotel resort who had called her *banjaaran*, and now this too fell into place. How strange life is, she thought. She never wanted to be a star, but her dad pushed her into it. On the other hand, her twin sister was desperate to be an actress and had to perform on beaches to try to satisfy her ambitions.

'I need to see her,' said Deepa decisively. 'I want to tell her that I didn't know she existed. It's not my fault our lives have developed the way they have.'

'It's late,' said Shankar. 'Let's get some rest and we can go to her tomorrow.'

The next day, as Shankar had vowed, he took Deepa to the travel agent and bought two flights to Goa. Deepa's parents had been phoning her frantically, but she refused to take their calls. She sent a text message to Sachin, explaining that she needed a few days to think and she then dialled Ajay's number.

'Deepa! I've been worried about you, why haven't you been answering your calls?'

'Long story Ajay, I can't talk for long now but I just wanted to tell you some good news… the stalker isn't a stalker after all. He's my grandpa.'

'What?'

'Yes, he's my grandfather. I still can't believe it… He's my dad's dad and I didn't even know that he was alive… It's a crazy, complex story Ajay and I'll tell you everything when you come back to Mumbai. I've got a few really important things to do and my brain's a bit fuzzy at the moment.'

'Gosh… I understand,' said Ajay. 'But I worry about you, please look after yourself.'

Deepa smiled. She could tell he cared about her. 'Make sure you call me as soon as you get back to Mumbai, Ajay. I'm going to need all the support I can get.'

'Of course I will babe. Take care.'

'Bye.'

At midday, Shankar and his granddaughter were on their way to the airport. Shankar felt terrible that Deepa had fallen out with her parents because of him, but he was also surprised to hear they'd kept everything secret from her and her brother. He was looking forward to seeing his grandson too, but knew that he would have to wait a while.

Deepa looked out of the window as the aeroplane took off, and watched as Mumbai got smaller and smaller. With the cars reduced to tiny specks and the buildings resembling something from a model village, she put her head back and closed her eyes.

'It's not all their fault,' said Shankar softly. He took Deepa's hand in his. 'Your dad made a mistake by gambling, it's true, but your uncle and I over-reacted. Then we all made an even bigger mistake by splitting the family up. None of us have ever been the same since,' admitted Shankar sadly. 'Whenever we looked at Neha, we wondered what you were like. It must have been even harder for your parents. They lost their little girl.'

'I'll never speak to them again,' Deepa declared coldly. 'What they've done is beyond forgiveness. Please don't talk about them.' And with that, she closed her eyes once more.

Soon they had landed in Goa, and at last Shankar's dream was about to come true. He would see both of his granddaughters side by side for the first time in seventeen years.

Chapter 10

As they drove from the airport in a taxi, Shankar pointed out the house he shared with Deepa's uncle, aunt and sister. But they didn't stop. Instead, the car carried on a mile up the road and pulled up by the beach.

Deepa was puzzled.

'Follow me, dear,' he said. 'It's that time of day.'

After a brief walk along the beach, Deepa realised what her grandfather meant. A hundred yards in the distance, a girl was dancing for a group of tourists – it was Deepa's double, her sister.

As they approached Neha, Deepa was astounded to see how much they resembled one another. But she also couldn't help thinking how beautiful her sister was. Neha was wearing a red *lehnga choli* with an intricate gold and green embroidered design. She had a tattoo on one side of her stomach and her long, dark curls cascaded down her back. Neha, with her extraordinarily well-toned figure, looked even more like a Bollywood superstar than she did, Deepa thought.

'The schoolchildren come every day,' Shankar said to Deepa as they stood together. 'We tell Neha she's too old for it now… hanging out with the local kids and dancing like this. She needs to grow up.'

Deepa watched in awe at her sister's performance.

She really was a sight to behold; Neha was both stunning and graceful. 'But she loves doing it, doesn't she?' said Deepa. 'Look at her, you can tell she's so comfortable with it… a natural.'

'Yes, she is and she also earns a fair bit here, especially in the holiday season. We don't touch a penny of it, though. She saves it… says she'll use it to move to Mumbai one day and become a star,' Shankar chuckled. 'Some of the tourists actually think she is the actress Deepa Khanna. They reckon you come all the way from Mumbai to perform on this beach. Neha thinks it's hilarious.'

'She's brilliant,' sighed Deepa. 'I'm not a great dancer but you can see it's effortless for Neha. She's doing this far better than I ever could.'

'Well, I won't be the judge of that, but she is fabulous,' agreed Shankar proudly. 'Although she's also very naughty. We were horrified when she disappeared to Mumbai without telling us,' he said with a hint of alarm in his voice. 'And then she caused all that trouble for you. I'm so sorry about that. God knows what got into her. Neha's father is still furious with her – they haven't spoken for days.'

'Really? That's too bad,' said Deepa, wondering whether Neha was also the person who'd broken into the hotel room.

'Yes, it is bad. And he doesn't know about the shoplifting incident yet. When the police turn up here to question Neha, all hell will break loose.'

'Don't worry about that,' said Deepa. 'Let me speak to Neha. If we both go to see the owner of the shop, they may even drop the charges. I know some very influential people,' she said, thinking of Ajay. 'If we can explain exactly what she was doing, and why, they may agree to let it go.'

Shankar gave Deepa a gentle pat on the back. 'You're a very sensible girl, you just need to pass some of that sense into your sister now,' he smiled. 'I'm proud of you, Deepa. Very proud. Your parents did a good job.'

Deepa looked down. She felt a twinge of sorrow at the mention of her parents but she didn't comment. She didn't want to spoil this moment.

'The song's finished. Let's go and speak to Neha, *Dadaji*,' Deepa urged. 'We've wasted enough time.'

Shankar's eyes welled up and he wiped away a tear with the tip of his finger and then dabbed his eyes with his shirt sleeve. Having her call him *Dadaji* made him feel like the happiest man on earth. 'Come on, *beti*,' he replied. 'Let's go.'

The two of them linked arms and walked a few more metres across the sand. It was a hot day and

Deepa dabbed her sticky forehead with a tissue. She was wearing high-heeled sandals, but could still tell that the sand beneath her feet was scorching. She wondered how Neha could dance in such heat and still look immaculate.

'Eh! Eh!' Neha yelled at one of the local schoolboys who had been watching her. 'Put that money back in the box!'

He was trying to make off with five rupees and thought Neha hadn't noticed.

'I have eyes in the back of my head,' she said as she walked around with her collection box. The onlookers happily parted with their spare coins.

Deepa and Shankar hung back until most people had dispersed. When just Neha and a few local boys remained, they decided to approach her. Neha was gleefully counting how much money she had made that afternoon but as soon as she clapped eyes on her grandfather with Deepa, the smile on her face disappeared.

'Neha *beti*, I have a surprise for you. I think it's time you met your sister.'

She cut her grandfather a glance that suggested she didn't think it was the best idea he'd ever had. Neha took a long look at Deepa then hastily began gathering her belongings together. She grabbed her

CD player that was perched on a wooden stool and her collection of CDs.

Some of the young lads who were still there recognised Deepa. They started whispering and giggling to one another, and one of them looked awe-struck.

'You lot go home!' shouted Neha when she saw their reaction. 'Entertainment's over for today, understand?' Realising she meant what she said, they scarpered.

Deepa saw that Neha wasn't going to be won over that easily, and so she decided to take the initiative. 'Neha, I'd like to talk to you.'

'And why's that then?' Neha responded flatly.

'Because you're my sister and I only discovered that you existed yesterday.'

'Oh really?'

'Really. I know you might find this hard to believe, but for some reason our parents felt it was best to hide the truth from me. You're lucky that nothing was kept from you.'

Deepa felt sad as she carried on talking. 'You knew about me, and you knew how and why we got separated. I didn't have a clue. I was happy in my world until yesterday. I'm distraught at discovering my whole life has been a lie.'

Neha twitched her nose. It was something she did when she was feeling nervous and edgy.

Sweeping aside some loose strands of hair, Deepa dared to take a few steps closer to her sibling. 'I mean what I say, Neha. I'd really like the chance to get to know you. This has been a shock for me but I know it's not your fault. Why should we have to suffer because of what they did to us?'

'Suffer?' said Neha bitterly. 'You, *suffer?*'

Deepa made no reply. She realised her sister had a lot of pent-up ill feelings about her and she obviously needed to get them off her chest.

'*You're* not the one who suffered. It was ME!' Neha spat out. '*You're* not the one who was raised by your uncle and aunt. *You're* not the one miming to Bollywood songs on a beach… YOU get to do them for real!'

'Neha!' reprimanded Shankar, shocked at the revelation that Neha had such feelings of resentment towards her uncle and aunt. 'You were brought up as lovingly as any child on this planet!' he said sternly. 'My son and daughter-in-law raised you as though you were their own biological child. They did everything to make sure you got everything you ever needed.'

'Yes, *Dadaji*, they did their best but they didn't

make me a star, did they?' snapped Neha. 'I'm not famous – she is,' she added, pointing at Deepa, 'because she was raised by her *real* mum and dad. They helped to turn her into a famous film star. I'm at college in the day and dancing like a fool on the beach. A poor *banjaaran*. Nothing more.'

Shankar's eyes welled up as he realised the extent to which Neha felt hard done by. He couldn't believe what he was hearing and it hurt him deeply.

But Neha didn't seem to care. She slung her CD player over her shoulder, slipped on her sparkly flip-flops and stalked off.

'Neha, please stop,' Deepa pleaded. She ran a few steps after her. 'I didn't choose to be the one who went to Mumbai. I didn't choose to be the star,' she added. 'I never even wanted stardom. I was kind of pushed into the movies by my dad… our dad.'

Neha stopped to listen but she refused to turn and look at Deepa.

'Dad made me do all this – I'm not even that brilliant at it,' said Deepa candidly. 'I can act, but I can't dance to save my life. I think you're amazing, and if you didn't get opportunities earlier maybe I can help you now.'

Neha turned around. 'What, you're going to pay me off so that you can feel less guilty?'

'No, Neha. I'm not going to pay you off. I'm not anywhere near as rich as you probably think,' she laughed. 'All I meant is that if you want to act, perhaps I can try to open some doors for you. I can introduce you to people who may be able to use you in their movies. But please don't be angry with me. I didn't know I had a sister, but you did. And you still never came looking for me…'

Deepa's voice started to crack and she pursed her lips together, as if that would help to contain all her emotions. But it was no good. The tears wouldn't wait, so Deepa held her hands up to her face instead. She was mortified to be pouring her heart out like this on a public beach, but she couldn't help herself.

Shankar moved forward and put his arms around Deepa. When he hugged her, he too felt his heart would explode.

As she was sobbing into her grandfather's arms, Deepa felt somebody's hand on her shoulder. She turned around and saw a woman she didn't recognise, but who obviously knew her.

'Oh my God!' the woman cried, extending her arms out to Deepa and squeezing her as tightly as she could. 'You don't know who I am, do you?' the lady asked.

Deepa shook her head.

'I'm your auntie. Neha's mum,' said the woman. 'My name is Sujata, and if you hadn't got ill I would have raised you,' she smiled lovingly. 'Instead, Neha became my daughter.'

'You sound disappointed that you got me, Mum,' said Neha as she watched the emotional reunion taking place in front of her.

'I'm not disappointed!' Sujata answered. 'I'm the happiest woman alive! My little niece has come back and my daughter has finally found her sister.'

'You may be happy to see me, Auntiji, but I don't think Neha feels the same way,' said Deepa sadly. 'I think I should go back home.'

'You can't go now,' said Sujata, taking her hand and gently cupping one side of Deepa's face. 'I've been waiting for years for this moment. I kept hoping all three of you would come back some day – you and your parents. Where have you been all these years?' she asked tearfully.

'Men are so stubborn and unforgiving. I told Neha's papa to forgive Jayant. I said over and over, let's go and find them, but no! Once they cut someone out of their lives, that's it. They don't care that the two little girls they separated were the ones who suffered the most.'

'She's right, Deepa,' said Shankar. 'I should have

intervened, and been stronger… you have all suffered far too much.'

'Neha had such a lonely childhood,' Sujata said sadly. 'We weren't able to give her any siblings so she grew up alone even though she had her own sister all along. It upsets me just to think about it.'

Neha stood watching from a distance as Sujata poured her heart out. 'Now Neha goes to the beach and dances like a gypsy girl, but she won't let us stop her. I only came here today because I realised she's late. You never know what can happen these days… But this stupid girl, does she listen? No.'

'She's a great dancer,' commented Deepa.

Neha flashed a look of surprise at her twin.

'Yes I know,' said Sujata. 'She's smart too – she's studying nursing. Your dad will be proud of her.'

'I don't care what that man thinks, Mum!' Neha suddenly burst out. 'It's his fault that our family was broken up in the first place!'

Deepa was taken aback by Neha's anger towards her father, and she found it hard to deal with. Even though Deepa was furious with him herself, to hear somebody else saying negative things about him made her feel defensive.

Perhaps Deepa had forgiven him already.

'You don't know how much Jayant has suffered,'

Sujata told Neha. 'He's your real father, he must have been devastated at having to leave you behind.'

'I doubt it,' Neha spat out. 'Anyway, who cares? Deepa's family doesn't even concern me.'

And with that, Neha turned her back on the three of them and walked away again.

'Not even your kid brother?' asked Deepa.

Neha stopped.

'You have a brother too,' Deepa informed her. 'His name is Sachin and he's the best brother anybody could hope for. He's not going to believe all this. I think he'd love to meet you, Neha.'

Neha didn't flinch. She stayed where she was, with her back towards them. She was obviously stunned by this news.

'You're still young, Neha. Don't let all this anger eat you up and ruin your life. You're only seventeen… You could become a star too,' Deepa went on. 'I may be signing up to a film where I have a double role to play. Perhaps I can persuade the producer to hire us both – people really will do a double take then!'

Neha finally turned around. She was grinning broadly. 'Come on then, Sis, follow me. Let's go back home and you can help me pack… we're going to Mumbai!'

About the author

Puneet Bhandal has worked in the publishing industry for many years as a writer and designer. She has extensive knowledge of the entertainment business especially Bollywood, having been a film journalist in the past where her work involved visiting film sets and interviewing actors, directors and producers.

Puneet is currently busy with her Bollywood Series books tour, appearing at schools, libraries and literary events across the UK. For more information, visit www.puneetbhandal.com or www.bollywoodseries.com

www.PuneetBhandal.com

Your thoughts...

'A *brilliant* sequel… there's so much going on in this book!' **Amisha, 12**

'I didn't know how it was going to end until I got there… really enjoyed it,' **Sara, 14**

'I had to keep reading to find out what was going to happen. I read it in three hours!' **Jas, 13**

'I really enjoyed the book and I can't wait for the next one! I had a Bollywood themed 11th birthday party this year and it was great fun! The real Bollywood sounds very exciting!!! I wish I could go one day,' **Eleanor, 11**

'Loved it, looking forward to book 3,' **Noreen, 10**

'I haven't read the book yet but it looks so good. But why isn't it in colour? The book looks so eye catching.' **Zoe, 11**

'I have recently been to the ASPIRE event at Uxbridge College and am reading *Starlet Rivalry* of the Bollywood Series and it is a page turner. Thank you.' **Fahim, 11**

Book order form

You can order further copies of this book direct from
Famous Books with FREE UK DELIVERY.

To order further copies of *Bollywood Series: Double Take*,
please send a copy of the form below to:

Famous Books
Orders Department
2 St Peters Rd
Southall
Middx UB1 2TL

Alternatively, visit www.bollywoodseries.com and
click on the 'Buy Me' link to order online and have
the book delivered direct to your door.

— — — — — — — — — — —

Please send me _____ copies of *Double Take*.

I enclose a UK bank cheque or postal order, payable to
Famous Books for _____ (at £5.99 per copy).

NAME
ADDRESS

POSTCODE
EMAIL

Please allow 14 days for delivery. Do not send cash. Offer subject to
availability. Please tick box if you do not wish to receive further
information from Famous Books ❑